BLIND
BRAG

Recent novels by John Wainwright:

John Wainwright
BLIND BRAG

St. Martin's Press
New York

Library in Congress Cataloging-in-Publication Data

Wainwright, John William, 1921-
    Blind brag / by John Wainwright.
        p.   cm.
    ISBN 0-312-01737-5 : $14.95
    I. Title.
PR6073. A354B53   1988
823' .914—dc19   87-38260
                                                      CIP

First published in Great Britain by Macmillan London Limited.

First U.S. Edition

10 9 8 7 6 5 4 3 2 1

SECOND
STAGE

Friday, October 20th

10.00 p.m.

Outside, the Rain Gods seemed to have negotiated some kind of bonus production agreement; the window was about level with the goose-neck lamps of the street lighting and the water was coming down in wind-gusted waves. It was always the same. Every year. Start ticking the days off towards Bonfire Night and all that wood and garbage the kids have collected for November the Fifth gets soaking wet.

Not that I am in favour of knocking Guy Fawkes every year. Guy Fawkes was a well-intentioned Yorkshireman who happened to be in the wrong place at the wrong time, and I know the feeling well. Half a century ago I did it myself and, anyway, I rather like fireworks. No doubt, come the day, loving fathers and favourite uncles would find enough paraffin and old sump oil to get the flames licking the dampness out of the pile, and then would come chestnuts and roasted potatoes and all the rest of it.

I hoped so.

On the other hand, I could have been wrong. The mental meanderings of modern youth had left me hanging on the golden bough of nostalgia years ago. In my day we used to burn better looking effigies than some of the kids I see slouching through school gates these days.

Maybe Bonfire Night wasn't around any more.

Quite suddenly I found I was not registering what I was reading. Even the hard-boiled poetry of Chandler was going in at the eyes but being stopped from reaching the

7

brain by a wall of once-upon-a-time. It seemed a pity to waste such good prose.

I glanced at the alarm clock, dropped the book on the bed and swung my feet onto the carpet. I needed company and a glass of nice, tangy cider would clear my taste-buds for the good-night beaker of hot chocolate.

One of the advantages of having an office-cum-living-quarters above a wine-bar-cum-restaurant is that you don't have far to go for food and drink. There is a second advantage if the wine-bar-cum-restaurant is owned and run by Bull Adams.

'Bull' because he was once an RSM in the Brigade of Guards. Within five minutes of meeting him you can make an educated guess. Within ten minutes he will have *told* you.

His life story since leaving the army is not very complicated. He 'retired' to live with his daughter and son-in-law at Rogate-on-Sands. Within six months he was bored to tears. The then rather sleazy wine-bar-cum-restaurant, with living quarters above, came up for sale. Adams took the plunge, kicked out the trollops and fairies, re-designed the place then, because he still wanted to live with his daughter, rented me the upper rooms.

And, because the Wine Bibber was a few hundred yards inland from the prom, the customers were mainly local. In October, with the holiday trade at least a month behind us, they were *only* local.

'Harry.' The middle-aged, motherly type Bull employed behind the bar nodded a greeting. 'The usual?'

'Cider,' I agreed.

'Bull reckons you have Devonshire blood in you.' It was draught cider and she drew it carefully. Maggie took great pride in her work. 'I reckon you just have the taste.'

'No Devonshire blood.' I smiled.

I paid her, sipped what might have been the over-spill

from the surface, then glanced around the main room. Bull was at one of the tile-topped tables. Lyle was sitting with him. Bull was enjoying his usual tipple: Guinness with a whisky chaser. Lyle had a half-consumed glass of bitter in front of him.

I carried my cider across and joined them.

Lyle was the local divisional detective chief inspector and, if the private-eye novels I enjoyed reading were to be believed, we should have shared a cat-and-dog life. We didn't. I think he tolerated me as a mild, but harmless eccentric. I, on the other hand, rather *liked* him and for a variety of reasons. In the first place, he neither looked nor talked like a policeman. He wasn't pushy, he wasn't arrogant and not once since I'd known him had he sneered at *my* chosen profession. On a couple of occasions – and off the record – he'd slipped me a little help.

In return I had kept well clear of constabulary corns. Whenever things had moved towards genuine illegality I had dutifully trotted along to the Rogate-on-Sands Police Station to make formal notification. .

It had not helped me to attract clients, but it had ensured a friendly smile from the local constabulary.

I lowered myself onto a chair and caught the last few words Bull was saying.

'. . . and it's what they need. A few times round Pirbright parade ground, at the double, *that*'s what they need. Discipline.'

Lyle raised his glass to his lips and glanced his gentle amusement in my direction.

'The present-day youth?' I conjectured.

'*You* know what I mean.' Bull turned to me for support. 'You were in the army.'

'National Service,' I reminded him. 'I was just about trying the boots for size when they de-rationed tea.'

'Korea,' growled Bull.

'I was there,' I agreed. 'Not for long . . . but I *was*

there. I can't say it was the most spiritual experience of my life.'

'Ah, but it made a *man* of you.'

'Did it?' I was deliberately being awkward. Bull-baiting was a gentle game some of us enjoyed and, with the proviso that nobody became too personal, Bull didn't seem to mind. I tasted the cider, and added, 'I was scared to death.'

'Of course. But you still . . .'

'I thought I'd caught gonorrhoea,' I ended.

Lyle lowered his glass and grinned. Bull compressed his lips in mock-outrage then tasted his stout and sipped at his whisky.

It was a pleasant enough way to end an unspectacular day. Beyond the shoulder-high partition the buzz of conversation from the diners still in the restaurant filtered through and formed a gentle acoustic back-drop. Only a handful of drinkers were at the bar side of the partition and none were near enough to eavesdrop.

Not that we said much worth listening to. Bull had taken his daughter's kids up the coast to see the Blackpool Illuminations.

'Twins,' he said, proudly. Anybody might have thought *he* was personally responsible.

Lyle teased, 'And, of course, Grandpa didn't enjoy the spectacle at all.'

'Not bad.' Bull gave an appreciative sideways nod of the head. 'It stretches the season out.'

'The Lancs County boys hardly have time to breathe.' Lyle showed appropriate sympathy for his colleagues in the neighbouring county. 'Conferences, the Illuminations, Christmas coming up fast. All that on top of the holiday season.'

'They shouldn't have joined.' Bull bounced the old sweat's standard comeback off Lyle's remark.

'By comparison,' I murmured, 'you must have a cushy number.'

'More often than not,' agreed Lyle. Then, with a smile, 'We have had our moments, of course.'

I nodded and enjoyed another taste of cider.

And that was when he told us about the amnesiac.

The man – name not known, age somewhere in the mid-twenties – had wandered into the police station in the early hours of that morning. Moderately well dressed, but without either mac or overcoat, and with at least a three-day growth of whiskers on his face. A still-bleeding wound which had required half-a-dozen stitches on the left cheek. Bruises on both forearms. He hadn't known who he was, hadn't known where he'd come from, hadn't known where he was making for. No means of identification; every pocket was empty. No record of his fingerprints; obviously he hadn't been processed by the police in the past.

'An accident?' I suggested.

'Nothing reported.'

'Hit-and-run, perhaps?'

'It's possible.' He sounded doubtful. 'The injuries aren't consistent with anything a motorist might drive away from.'

'A mugging,' offered Bull. 'If the pockets were empty.'

'I may be wrong, but I wouldn't buy it.' Lyle drank some more of his beer. 'Muggers don't take *everything*. He hadn't even a handkerchief.'

'So now,' I said, 'you're left with masterly inactivity. You sit on him until he's reported Missing from Home.'

'The Memorial Hospital,' Lyle corrected me. 'Specifically, the Andrew Fryer Ward. When he's rested – assuming *we* haven't come up with the answer – the funny farmers are going to poke around a little.'

'God help the man,' growled Bull.

10.45 p.m.

God help the man, indeed.

I knew what psychiatrists and psychologists were like. I knew from personal experience. That unholy trio, Freud, Jung and Adler had a lot to answer for. Some few years ago pressure of work chasing impossible scoops for one of the top provincial rags had knocked some of *my* clockwork out of sync. The mind-benders had put me right but, in the process, had built the firm foundations for an unemployed hack heading straight for a divorce court.

I had ridden *that*, too. But what it had all done for my self-confidence I shuddered to think.

Therefore as I left the Wine Bibber my thoughts – and my sympathy – revolved around this unknown chap upon whom the shrinks were to be let loose.

I have already remarked that I hadn't far to go. Out of Bull's place, sharp left and there was my own front door, leading to the stairs up which clients had to trudge to reach the domain of the Thompson Detective Bureau. It was there, on the brass plate by the door. What it didn't say was that I was 'it'. I was cook, bottle-washer, sweeper-up, office-boy, stamp-licker . . . everything. I was 'Thompson' and I was also the 'Detective Bureau'. The rooms at the front were the Waiting Room and Office. The rooms at the rear were my bed-sit, my bathroom and my minuscule kitchen.

So, why a private detective?

Allow me to answer the question before you ask it, because you certainly *will* ask it . . . eventually. Everybody does.

Investigative journalism was, I thought – and still think – the ideal grounding for detective work. Better than try-ing door knobs. Better than directing traffic. Detectives ask questions. So do investigative journalists. But few de-tectives have the gall to ask the sort of questions which

12

expose a Poulson or (to quote the extreme example) push a President from the White House. Only the IJ crowd can slam *that* sort of question into the face of some outwardly respectable citizen.

I was, therefore, going to be a truly hot-shot private detective.

It did not work out that way.

The big firms had already cornered the market. They had the gadgetry, they had round-the-clock-seven-days-a-week service, they had a long-time reputation. They had everything, including the clients – the insurance companies, the industrial giants – with money enough to pay retaining fees.

All *I* had was myself, plus the few crumbs that fell from the table: parents, unhappy that their kid might be buying dope; some wife seeking evidence enough to bring a divorce; some back-street firm worried about trade-union extremists threatening to bring on bankruptcy.

The realisation that I was not going to make a fortune soon dawned, but I was happy enough. Liz and I remained friends – even *good* friends – and, unlike most ex-wives, she wasn't out to take the skin from my bones; she was qualified to sit behind a desk in one of the town's top solicitor's offices, therefore her income left mine at the foot of the hill; she knew this and, in lieu of what little alimony she might have squeezed from me, she was content with an evening out and dinner at one of the better eating spots once a month or thereabouts. When things became too tight Bull allowed the rent for the rooms to stay on the table pending better days and, more than once, he'd asked me down to the Wine Bibber as his guest for a meal.

It was all very civilised. Perhaps a little too civilised. More than once I'd pondered upon my good fortune in having so many people around to throw out life-lines. Had I been given the straight option of swimming or drowning I might have pushed myself a little harder.

On the other hand, I had no wish to drown.

That was the situation, then, as I kept an eye on the milk in the saucepan prior to making my last drink of the day. I also allowed my mind to touch upon the man Lyle had talked about.

Amnesia. (I'd looked it up before I'd started making the hot chocolate.) The inability to remember. It could be total or partial. If only partial it could cover a time, a place or an experience. It could be retro-active; like a door in the memory being slammed and everything beyond that door being closed off.

The book of words also insisted that retro-active amnesia rarely lasts longer than hours and *never* more than seven days. Anything more than a week and the diagnosis should be hysteria.

Thus the textbook I had at hand and, if the same textbook was available at the Memorial Hospital, the shrinks would be falling over each other to prove the poor chap crazy.

The milk simmered and began crawling up the inside of the pan. I took it from the jet and poured it onto the powdered chocolate in the pint-sized beaker. I turned off the jet and carried the drink into the bed-sit to cool while I undressed.

As I straightened the divan bed I caught a glimpse of the Chandler I'd been reading earlier. *The Big Sleep*. It seemed a strangely appropriate title.

Saturday, October 21st

9.30 a.m.

The Memorial is one of those hospitals built to discourage malingering. It is a dark-brick, two-storey pile; a ten-ward, Victorian monstrosity which seems to scowl disapproval at anybody with the impertinence to be ill. It has a half-moon, gravel drive to and from the porticoed entrance and, where modern hospitals might have lawns, The Memorial has a jungle of laurel.

It is a most depressing place.

On an impulse I had telephoned Lyle at his home and asked that I might visit the stranger who'd lost his memory.

'Why?'

'An unofficial, friendly approach.' It had seemed as good an excuse as any. 'It might help.'

'We haven't been *unfriendly*.'

'No . . . I wasn't suggesting that. But . . .'

'We haven't much choice when it comes to being "official".'

'That's what I mean.'

'You think he might have some deep, psychological hatred of policemen?'

'I didn't say that.'

'It might help.' He had seemed to reach a decision. 'It can't do any harm. There's a constable with him, in case he *is* somebody we want to lay our hands on. I'll give him a ring and tell him to let you have free rein.'

'Thanks. I'll let you know if I come up with anything.'

'But of course.'

And now I was crunching my way across the loose gravel and almost at the entrance to The Memorial.

Question – why on earth was I concerning myself with some stranger who didn't know who he was or whence he'd come?

Curiosity, I suppose. Perhaps because I wanted to prove that I was a genuine 'detective'. To prove it to myself, if not to other people. But mainly, I think, because that

15

strange sixth sense developed by all investigative journalists was nudging me in the ribs. Much as a good gun dog can sniff out game an IJ can feel when something is not quite kosher. He *knows* . . . but, at first, he doesn't know *why* he knows.

With surprise almost amounting to shock I realised that I was missing the excitement of following up gossamer-thin leads, of interviewing frightened people at secret meeting places, of building up an exposure strong enough to enmesh some lying, pseudo-respectable scoundrel in the filament of his own trickery.

We – the investigative journalists – were the trained skirmishing party, out ahead of the army of established law-enforcement. We identified and exposed the enemy, then stood aside while the heavier troops carried out the final annihilation.

But (I reminded myself) I was no longer an investigative journalist. I was a private detective. I was very much a solo performer.

I knew my way to the Andrew Fryer Ward and, when I reached it, I found the man I was there to see up and finishing an after-breakfast cup of coffee. He was wearing hospital pyjamas and a hospital dressing-gown. Both were at least three sizes too small and this did not add to his general appearance. His hair was as untidy as a vandalised bird's nest and the stitched-together lips of his cheek wound added to the overall picture of a man whose dignity had taken a severe battering.

The constable looked far too young to be wearing the uniform.

He moved a hand in a half-salute, and said, 'The chief inspector said you'd be coming, Mr Thompson.'

I nodded.

'If I can help, at all . . .'

'I don't think so.' Then, as an after-thought, I asked, 'What name does he answer to?'

'We don't know. That's why . . .'

'No. I mean what name are you *using*? Presumably you've progressed beyond the "Hey you" stage.'

'Well – er . . .' The constable moved his shoulders. 'Nothing, really. We've – y'know – been able to manage without.'

'I will,' I decided, 'call him Smith. Tom Smith.'

'Yes, sir.'

'Agreed?' I turned to the man I had just christened.

A shy, half-smile curved his lips for a moment and he gave a tiny nod.

'You are,' I reminded him quietly, 'a member of the human race. You are entitled to a name. If not your own, at least a temporary one.'

'Thank you.'

The constable said, 'If there's nothing else, sir . . .'

'I don't think so.'

'I'll – er – I'll nip outside for a cigarette. They're very hot on No Smoking in this place.'

'On your way out,' I said, 'have a quick word with the ward sister. Use what weight you have, plus the vicarious authority of Chief Inspector Lyle. We'd like the privacy of her office, if she doesn't mind.'

'I'll fix it, sir.'

The constable left us. He seemed rather pleased. It may have been that he was anxious to smoke a cigarette. Or it may have been that he was looking forward to a quasi-official tangle with the ward sister.

I glanced around the ward. Three beds were occupied. One held a middle-aged man with earphones clamped to his head. A younger man was sitting up, apparently immersed in the contents of a newspaper. The third man – an old and pinched-faced figure – was on his back with his mouth slightly open, snoring gently.

Perhaps all three were minding their own business. But perhaps not. The presence of a uniformed constable must have aroused some degree of curiosity. I was not prepared to take a chance.

I turned to the man I'd decided to call Tom Smith and said, 'Let's get you tidied up a bit. Then we'll seek what privacy we can find.'

I felt in my pocket, handed him my comb, then followed him as he padded from the ward and into the adjoining bathroom. I waited until he'd combed his hair into reasonable shape then led the way to the ward-sister's office.

It was the usual nursing-sister's bolt-hole. A deal more cheerful and airy than the ward. The desk was neat and uncluttered. The blotting-pad without a stain. On top of the steel filing cabinet was a vase of chrysanthemums. At one corner of the desk there was a glass ashtray; it was gleaming and without the hint of stain from use, but it was *there* and, as far as I was concerned, it meant that the No Smoking edict did not extend to this office.

We settled into the chain-store armchairs and I offered Tom Smith an opened packet of cigarettes. He took one and I thumbed my lighter and held the flame first to his cigarette then to my own.

'You've had a shave,' I observed.

'Yes.' He almost touched his cheek, but stopped in time. 'Except for the cut. I'll have to wait until that heals.'

'How many stitches?'

'Six.'

'From a knife . . . presumably?'

'I don't know.' A look of mild panic clouded his eyes. 'I don't remember *anything*.'

But I was remembering. I wasn't yet sure of what it *was* I was remembering, merely that I was getting used to the hospital garb and, since he'd straightened his hair, this Tom Smith was becoming somebody I should know. Not a stranger. At least, not *quite* a stranger.

I performed a mental juggling act. I tried to divide my

concentration between the conversation and the dredging of my memory *for* a memory.

'I'm not police,' I said.

'Oh.'

'Nor,' I added, hurriedly, 'am I from the mind-bending crowd.'

'That's a relief.' He managed a shy smile and drew on the cigarette.

'Just somebody trying to help.'

'I hope you've some success.'

The voice was that of an educated man but the third vowel hinted at somewhere north of the border.

'Scotland?' I suggested.

'I beg your pardon?'

'Just the hint of an accent. I think you're from Scotland, or you've lived a long time there.'

'I'm afraid I . . .' He moved a hand in a helpless gesture. 'I can't help.'

'You found a police station,' I reminded him.

'It would seem so.'

'Recognised it as such.'

'Where else? I mean, where *else* do you go when you're − y'know . . . like me.'

'A child wouldn't go there,' I teased, quietly. 'A child who hadn't been *taught*. Who didn't *know*.'

'No.' He frowned. 'I see your point.'

'How old are you?' I switched the direction of my questions quite deliberately.

'I don't know. Twenty-five. Twenty-six. Something like that.'

'Which university?'

'Have I *had* a university education?'

'At a guess.'

'It's possible,' he sighed.

'Therefore,' I murmured, '*a posse ad esse.*'

19

'Quite.' His expression changed and he breathed, 'From the possible to the actual.'

'You know Latin,' I nodded.

'Schoolboy Latin.' He suddenly looked eager. Almost happy.

'Schoolboy Latin,' I agreed. 'But, how do you *know* it's schoolboy Latin?'

Some of the eagerness left his expression and he shook his head.

Meanwhile one part of my brain was flicking through a whole gallery of faces. Television stars and personalities. Stage and screen people. Authors whose photographs I'd glimpsed on dustjackets. Musicians, painters, entrepreneurs. I'd met a lot of people; as a journalist it had been part of my job to meet people. I knew the faces of even more. Hundreds – thousands – of faces and, somewhere in the past, I might have glimpsed the face of this Tom Smith. No . . . not 'might have'. I was almost sure I *had*.

'The cut on your cheek.' I continued my probing. 'Six stitches. It must have been bleeding badly.'

'Yes.'

'What time did you arrive at the police station?'

'One o'clock. Two o'clock. Thereabouts.'

'Yesterday morning.'

He nodded.

'Rogate-on-Sands,' I mused. 'We have more than our fair share of hotels. Good-class. Medium-class.'

'I don't see what . . .'

'The majority of the staff don't live in,' I explained. 'There's little industry in these parts. A whole chunk of the population are employed as cleaners, waiters, bar-people. The backroom personnel needed to keep these places running. It's out of season, but we have conferences. Lots and lots of conferences. There's steady, all-year-round employment for most of the hotel workers.'

'You're getting at something, but I don't know what.'

20

'They work all hours,' I explained. I drew on my cigarette then tapped ash into the ashtray. I continued, 'The hotel people. Those places don't keep themselves cleaned and polished without a fair amount of out-of-sight activity. Usually at night. And the police station is there, between the sea front and the main residential district. Somebody *must* have seen you.'

'At *that* hour?' He didn't sound convinced.

'Tom Smith, old son.' I smiled what I hoped was genuine friendship. 'I know this town. It's never *busy* . . . like Leeds, like Birmingham. But, it's never completely dead. Every few minutes there's a taxi driving past. A car. A cyclist. There's always *somebody*. Going to work or coming away from work. There's *always* somebody.'

'You think I was seen?' It was a flat and unhappy question.

' I think you *must* have been seen.' I did not have to put certainty into the words. I *was* certain. I said, 'A few days' growth of beard. I take it your clothes were dirty . . .'

'They're being cleaned at the moment.'

'. . . and, on top of all that, a slash on the cheek needing six stitches. Blood all over the place. Somebody *must* have noticed you.'

'People mind their own business,' he said, sadly.

'Do they?' I narrowed my eyes a little. 'And where,' I asked, 'did you learn *that* opinion?'

'What?'

'That's the sort of remark a townie makes. Country people – yokels from the sticks – *don't* mind their own business. They're very nosey. Even at a place like this. The Rogate-on-Sanders work up a fair head of steam when something unusual happens. Even something only *mildly* unusual. Give them a stranger wearing dirty clothes, sporting a face that hasn't seen a razor for the best part of a week, wandering around the streets spilling blood all over their beautiful, tree-lined streets . . . the telephone wires would have been really humming. You wouldn't have had to *find* the police station. A squad car would have picked you up before you'd walked a hundred yards.'

There was much of the same stuff. Nit-picking away at trivialities. Trying to kick-start this Tom Smith character into remembering *something*. It was like trying to hand-catch a flying sparrow; his answers seemed to swoop and dive and curve away leaving only annoyance and disappointment.

We were at it for more than an hour and, at the end of that time, his face had a fixed expression of sad hopelessness.

And, yet . . .

Somewhere in there a tiny bell had given a barely audible ring. I'd knocked one feather from the sparrow's wing but, for the life of me, I couldn't identify it.

I stood up and squashed my second cigarette into the ashtray.

'That's enough for one day,' I said.

'Will you come again?'

'Why not?'

'I'd like *somebody* to visit me. I'd like to know *somebody* I can call a friend.'

There was a depth of loneliness in the remark. It said just about everything there was to say about complete amnesia.

I touched his upper arm as I left, and promised, 'I'll be back.'

2.30 p.m.

I could have gone to his office, but Lyle had suggested we meet in one of the shelters on Rock Walk. It was a crazy meeting-place. The open front faced west and, beyond the soaked grass of the gardens and the slight barrier of the rocks which gave the walk its name, the Irish Sea hammered the base of the promenade with God knows how many million tons of raging water. It was high tide and something of a gale was brewing up. The spray danced high in the air and, occasionally, 10p-sized gobs of the stuff flew into the shelter. We both sat, half-turned and facing each other, and we almost had to shout to make ourselves heard above the steady roar of the wind.

'Anything?' asked Lyle.

'Not a lot. He's obviously used to smoking cigarettes. I offered him one and he didn't cough his heart up.'

'Not a lot,' agreed Lyle.

'He knows which way to part his hair.'

'Ah!'

'And I think he's from Scotland.'

'I noticed the slight accent.'

'He knows Latin,' I shouted.

'Does he, indeed?'

'I'm not suggesting he's a Latin scholar, but he recognised a Latin tag I slipped into the conversation.'

'Clever.' Lyle nodded.

'He answers to the name of Tom Smith.'

'Good God!' Lyle looked surprised.

'That's not his real name, of course.' I smiled as I snatched back the toffee-apple Lyle thought I'd given him. 'I had to call him *something*. I chose Tom Smith, and he seems happy enough.'

Lyle hesitated, then asked, 'Do you know him?'

'Why? Should I?'

'I don't know.' He frowned. 'I have that feeling. That I've seen him somewhere before.'

I stopped myself from saying anything and waited.

Lyle continued, 'A feeling that I *should* know him. That's what I mean.' He scowled as he tried to be more precise. 'You pass somebody in the street. You do a double-take because you think you know them, then realise you *don't*

23

know them. Then you spot their name as somebody appearing in a show up the coast at Blackpool, perhaps. Then you realise you *do* "know" them . . . but not personally. Does that make sense?'

'It makes sense,' I assured him. 'If you *do* come up with the name, let me know.'

'Why?' He smiled.

'Eh?'

'Once he's been identified, that's the end of the matter.'

Despite the voice, raised to counter the rush of the wind, there was a saccharine sweetness in the tone. Quite suddenly I did not altogether trust this Detective Chief Inspector Lyle.

7.45 p.m.

Liz had one of those gold nail-guards on the index finger of her left hand. They were becoming very fashionable and, used with the right shade of varnish, they were rather sexy. Liz was using the right shade of nail varnish.

I didn't ask her who had bought it. I knew. Liz was strictly 'professional' and her profession was the law. She had no sugar daddy in the background. Nor (I was sure) had she any men friends likely to splash out on a trinket like that.

I was sure.

I was so sure that I fished!

'Nice,' I remarked, nodding at it against the white table-cloth.

'I like it.' She lifted the finger about an inch, then let it fall.

'Real gold?'

'Of course.'

'I won't ask who bought it.'

'You just *have*,' she grinned. '*I* bought it, if you

must know. I liked the look of it . . . so I bought it.'

I relaxed a little.

Liz is the only woman I know who can actually grin. I mean *grin*. It goes well beyond a smile and in no way resembles a smirk. It is not a grimace. It is no mere exposure of white and even teeth. It is a grin . . . and nothing more.

We were the product of a present-day civilisation. As an investigative reporter and a highly qualified solicitor we were about neck-and-neck in the educational stakes; what she lacked in worldly experience I more than made up for in a tendency towards the inability to be bothered with some of the minutiae of everyday living. It had seemed a good idea to marry.

It had *not* been a good idea.

The chemistry for a good marriage had not been there. The day-in-day-out patience of accepting annoying little habits as being part of the package deal. Neither of us could do it. My habit of jotting notes on the back of used envelopes brought the glint of battle into her eyes. Her habit of *always* pointing out every road sign when *I* was driving just about drove me up the wall. She could never remember that I always took my coffee black. I could never remember that she always smoked tipped cigarettes.

Basically, it was both simple and ridiculous. We were crazy about each other but our respective personalities prevented us from living together with any degree of harmony.

After my breakdown we'd talked it over in a very calm – very unemotional – manner. No blame. Neither asked the other to alter. A mutually acceptable divorce . . . and see how things went from there. But let us remain friends.

Which is what we were. Friends – good friends – who occasionally slept together.

That was our story. Correction . . . that was *her* story. *My* story included self-recrimination and the sort of sadness a man who's let gold dust run through his fingers rather than clench his fist might feel.

'I think Dover sole.' She closed the menu and handed it across the table. 'Dover sole, with trimmings.'

'Twice.' I did not touble to open the menu. The Beaconsfield was a good hotel. It ran one of the best restaurants in town. The food was *always* delicious.

The waiter jotted down the order, the wine waiter arrived and, again, I let Liz choose, then we waited and, for a few minutes, said nothing.

In the background, and very softly, big-band music filled in the gaps between the general conversation of the restaurant. You had to listen carefully to catch Dorsey's 'Song of India'. That, too, was something we tended to disagree about. Those bands of the thirties and forties played my sort of music. The Dorseys, Goodman, Shaw, James, Henderson. They'd never been equalled for a combination of brilliant section-work woven behind individual solo spots.

Liz liked the modern classics. Her musical taste-buds were sweetened by Britten, Mahler, Shostakovich and Delius. Those and some I did not even count important enough to remember. Liz would go dreamy-eyed. I ended up with a mild headache.

'You're very thoughtful this evening,' she observed.

I'd been straining to catch Dorsey's trombone slide in for the final few phrases but, instead, I smiled and said, 'A man I call "Tom Smith". Nobody knows his real name. Even *he* doesn't know.'

She seemed interested and I told her the story.

I ended by saying, 'Lyle. You've met him a few times in court.'

'Quite a few times.'

'And?'

'As a police officer, or as a witness?'

'Both.'

'Very honest. Very clever.' She paused, then said, 'He knows how to use honesty for his own ends.'

I looked puzzled.

'He can tell a truth,' she explained, 'then follow it up with a second truth that completely demolishes the first.'

'How?'

'A simple example. In the witness box give an accused man credit for being a good husband. A good father. Then, in the next breath, show him to be an incorrigible liar. It's a courtroom trick and Lyle can play it with more variations than any other man I know.'

'Not to be trusted?' I made it a question, if only because forensic back-flips were things I knew little about.

'To be trusted, completely,' she contradicted. 'Merely that every truth he tells is told with a reason.' The grin lit up her face again as she added, 'Our Mr Lyle is far too clever to be caught out in an obvious fib.'

Wednesday, October 25th

3.45 p.m.

The Sunday was spent keeping an eye on the rear of premises which formed part of one of the parades of shops. The owner of a DIY store was worried that one of his employees had developed the habit of nipping back on the sabbath and helping himself to stock. Quite a lot of stock. We'd discussed it the previous Wednesday and decided that a key (or a duplicate key) was the means of gaining access. Unfortunately the only employee with a key was also the owner's favourite nephew, and uncle didn't want the police dragged in.

Sunny Jim duly arrived shortly after dark. I allowed him time to load a couple of hundred quid's worth of loot into the boot of the car, then stepped on-stage to play the heavy.

Being a 'private investigator' was as easy as falling off a log.

Monday morning had seen the great confrontation act in uncle's office. Uncle was annoyed with his light-fingered nephew but delighted with the Thompson Detective Bureau. He asked what he owed, I told him and he paid, in cash, on the spot. Nobody mentioned a receipt and it seemed only decent to ease the burden on the Inland Revenue and HM Customs and Excise by not mentioning the transaction. Uncle had had his problem solved, Sunny Jim was mildly relieved that he wasn't going to land up in court, and I had a few spare banknotes in my pocket.

Everybody was happy.

I'd taken the car in for an overdue service in the afternoon and had strolled to the end of Rogate-on-Sands pier pending somebody changing the oil, checking the tyre pressure and hitting the engine with a hammer in appropriate places.

And I'd thought about friend Tom Smith.

I had reached certain very firm conclusions.

He really was *not* my pigeon. I was human enough – humane enough, if you like – to sympathise, but that was as far as it went. That was as far as it *could* go. He wasn't some stray dog I could adopt and give a home to. That lonely-and-lost-in-a-storm look I had last seen on his face was very fetching, and he was obviously the sort of man with whom one could hold an intelligent conversation but, merely because his instant-recall mechanism was on

28

the blink, that was no basis upon which to build some sort of blood-brother relationship. I had my own worries. I might – I just *might* – call in for a short chat if he was still in The Memorial in a few days' time. But that was the limit.

That decision had been reached on the Monday.

Tuesday (it being the third Tuesday of the month) had seen me driving inland to the Pullbury and Norton Rifle and Pistol Club. Some men go for golf. Some men go for chess. Some men go for photography. My relaxation was target practice and the 'Pull and Nor' was one of the best gun clubs in the North-West. Its ranges and galleries were rarely unoccupied and, to make sure I never had a wasted journey, I had a permanent booking for the third Tuesday of every month.

I had my own weapon (a Walther) which the law required I keep locked away in the club's security room, but I also liked to fire one of the club's rifles. The occasional session with a revolver made for variety and I'd even blasted away with pump-action shotguns.

I counted the 'Pull and Nor' as the one indulgence of my life. Club fees and the cost of ammunition being what they are I could afford it . . . just. I argued that it put an edge on my concentration; match shooting, with either a handgun or a rifle demanded undiverted attention. Liz argued that it was noisy, a waste of time and money and nothing more than a silly, male ego-trip.

Perhaps there was a bit of both.

What Liz could never understand was the club-room side of things. There was a Ladies' Section – and, in honesty, some of the women members could nick the bull with annoying regularity – there was a Mixed Section – the main part of the club where married members brought their wives or girl-friends and where sex equality was absolute – and there was a Stag Section. I stayed with the Stag Section. We were the smallest section of the three but (we claimed) we included the best marksmen of the club in our number.

The Stag Section (like the Ladies' Section) had its own tiny annexe from the main club-room and, as a rule, that was where I spent much of my monthly visit to the 'Pull and Nor'. It was cosy. It had its own tiny, open fire, its own coffee machine and its own opening to the bar. It had deep armchairs, a scattering of side-tables and a selection of carefully chosen magazines with which to while away the time between shooting sessions. *The Shooting Times*, *The Field* and *The Countryman* were always there with, now and again, an occasional copy of some lesser-known publication. And, yesterday, one I hadn't seen before: *International Construction*.

That was where I saw a photograph of him. My 'Tom Smith' character.

I'd been leafing through this new magazine, wondering what on earth there was in this highly specialised publication which might interest gun buffs, when I'd spotted his photograph. He'd been one of a group at some sort of presentation ... and it had been a very *good* photograph.

Alex Campbell. Younger son of Sir Douglas Campbell, director general of the Burns Civil Engineering Group.

I'd torn the page from the magazine, driven back to Rogate-on-Sands, visited the main library and hunted around in the Reference Section.

Burns Civil Engineering Group. Holding company for Burns Bridge Construction, Burns Motorway Engineers, Burns Dam Projects, Burns Quarry and Mining Engineers. Those were the main companies. Almost a dozen lesser companies handled smaller stuff, like housing estates, land reclamation and the like. It would seem that the Burns boys could handle just about anything from dry rot to rising damp.

The holding company had a London registered office

and the registered office had a telephone number. I had left the library, returned to my bed-sit and telephoned the number.

The switchboard girl had said, 'Burns Civil Engineering. Can I help you?'

'I'd like to speak to Sir Douglas Campbell . . .'

'Who's calling, please?'

'It wouldn't mean anything.'

'Hold the line. I'll put you through to his secretary.'

After a pause, a high-class female voice had said, 'Sir Douglas Campbell's office.'

'I'd like to speak to Sir Douglas Campbell, please.'

'I'm his secretary. Can I help you?'

'I doubt it.'

'Can you state your business, please?'

'Not to you, lady.'

'Can you give me your name, please?'

I'd given her my name.

'And your address, please.'

I'd given her my address.

'And your telephone number, please.'

I'd given her my telephone number, then added, 'If it oils the rusty routine a little, I wish to speak about his son, Alex. That much I'll tell you . . . but no more.'

The pause had been a shade too long before she'd said, 'I'm afraid Sir Douglas isn't here at the moment. But I'll pass your message on to him at the first opportunity.'

And then she'd rung off.

That had been yesterday and now I'd opened the door of the bed-sit to a man who, on the face of things, could quietly quarter me with his bare hands and toss each quarter through a separate window.

'Won't you come in,' I said.

It was a little late. He already *was* in.

'Dilton-Emmet.' The voice went with the man. It was like a muffled roll on a timpani.

31

'I don't know anybody called . . .'

'That's *my* name, squire.'

'Oh! I'm . . .'

'I already know what *your* name is.'

'Oh!'

This character was quite new to my experience. I'd seen big men before but never one who *looked* as big. He topped the six foot mark by a few inches and his breadth of shoulder was in perfect proportion. The hooked nose would not have shamed the American eagle and the full set of whiskers, like the full shock of hair, were golden bronze liberally streaked with silver. In *any* company this man would have stood alone.

The divan creaked mild protest as he lowered himself into a sitting position.

'Yesterday,' he growled, 'you telephoned Sir Douglas Campbell.'

'I don't see what . . .'

'I made a statement. I didn't ask a question.'

'I *tried* to telephone him,' I admitted.

'Something about Alex, his son.'

'Something about Alex,' I agreed.

'*What* about Alex?'

'Oh, no.' I shook my head. 'You barge in here – Dilton-Emmet, I don't know who the hell you are – and you apparently expect me to take you at face value. No way, my friend. I need proof. Positive identification. *And* from Campbell.'

He chuckled. The impression was that the ornaments rattled.

He picked up the telephone, held it towards me and said, 'You know the number. You used it yesterday.'

'Some plummy-voiced female.'

'This time ask for Extension Four-One-Two-Three.'

I did and a man's voice said, 'Campbell here.'

'Sir Douglas Campbell?'

'Speaking.'

The big man leaned forward and covered the mouth-piece with his paw.

'Not *your* name,' he rumbled.

I nodded understanding and, when he'd cleared the mouthpiece, said, 'I have a man here who seems to think he represents you.'

'Describe him, please.' My words had not caused surprise.

'Big, bearded and very sure of himself.'

'Ask him to say something.'

'To you?'

'No. To *you*.'

I frowned perplexity then looked at the big man.

'He says you've to *say* something.'

'Tell him I refuse to make a fool of myself.'

'He refuses to make a fool of himself.'

'Good.' I heard what might have been a sigh of relief along the wire. Then, 'Trust him, please,' and the phone went dead.

I stared at the receiver before slowly replacing it on its cradle.

The big man had fished a packet of cheroots from his inside pocket. Long, slim, black cheroots. He chose one, then lighted it before he spoke.

'Well?' he asked.

'He said I should trust you.'

'Good.' He blew a cloud of particularly evil-smelling tobacco smoke in my direction.

'Whoever "he" is,' I added.

'Sir Douglas Campbell . . . surely?'

'A disembodied voice,' I corrected him. I scowled passing displeasure. 'I have the distinct feeling that I've knocked the lid from a very strange can of worms.'

'It *was* Campbell,' he assured me. 'You said all the right

things. That I refused to make a fool of myself. That was the agreed reaction.'

'A strange reaction.'

'The code-phrase – proof that I *am* here – if you prefer to be melodramatic.'

'My preference – if you're really interested – is to know what the hell's going on.' I did nothing to hide my irritability. 'This Tom Smith character.'

'Who?'

'. . . this man I now find is actually Alex Campbell. Until a couple of days ago I didn't know him from Adam. And *now* . . .'

The irritability was fuelling itself towards anger and I closed my mouth in mid-sentence.

'We started on the wrong foot, Thompson.' Nothing seemed to faze the big man. He relaxed on one elbow and the divan made another creaking protest. He raised the cheroot to his lips and thickened the atmosphere of the bed-sit a little more, then said, 'Let's start with your side of things. When did you first meet Alex?'

I told him. I made it a straightforward yarn; starting with Lyle's first mention of the man with amnesia and ending with my recognition of Alex Campbell in *International Construction*. I expressed no opinion and made no comment.

'Why not tell Lyle who he is?' asked the big man.

'I don't know.' It was the truth. It was also the truth when I added, 'I was an investigative reporter. Used to playing every card close to the chest. It's a habit.'

'You don't like Lyle? Don't trust him?'

'I don't *know* him enough. He's the divisional detective chief inspector. That's all I know about him. My wife . . .'

'Your *ex*-wife,' he interrupted bluntly and, when I

34

stared, he added, 'We do our homework very thoroughly, Thompson.'

'My *ex*-wife,' I said, tightly, 'tells me he's cunning, but honest.'

'He'd like that.' The bass-drum chuckle seemed to make the walls vibrate slightly. 'He'd appreciate that assessment.'

'Do you know him?'

'Unofficially.'

I'd said my piece. Or, at least, I'd said all I intended to say. I lighted a cigarette and added to the smoke-content of the room. I had this hunch – this tingling of the scalp – but now it was the turn of this Dilton-Emmet character to add something to the kitty.

He raised the stakes considerably.

'You're a private detective,' he rumbled.

'Yes.'

'A one-man-band.'

'Until I get established.'

'How much does it cost to hire you?'

I told him.

'A thousand pounds a day,' he murmured. Then added, 'Plus expenses.'

'Is – is that an offer?'

'Campbell needs your help.'

'Badly, by the sound of things.'

'Take it or leave it, Thompson. I'm not here to haggle.'

I organised my thoughts for a few moments, then said, 'It's illegal. Whatever it is, it's illegal. It *has* to be, at that price.'

'Not illegal. Dangerous, perhaps ... but not illegal.'

'Dangerous enough to be lethal.'

'For a thousand pounds a day?' The question had a distinct curled-lip quality. 'Thompson, a handful of the world's top entertainers can command four or five times that amount

35

for a couple of hours on a stage . . . and you can neither sing *nor* dance.'

He had not answered my implied question but, as I later learned, that was Dilton-Emmet. His personality was as big as his frame. Big enough to make you believe anything he wanted you to believe.

I felt slightly deflated as I asked, 'Okay, what am I expected to do?'

'Keep your mouth shut. That gets priority over everything.'

'It goes with the job,' I reminded him.

'Carry a parcel from Point A to Point B.'

I was no Einstein, but I was no fool. I think at that point in the conversation I could already have made an educated guess. But it would have *been* a guess, therefore I waited.

'Kidnapping,' he said, bluntly.

I nodded. It would have been a correct guess.

'Alex and his younger sister, Mary.'

'Alex?'

This time, he nodded.

'So, he *isn't* . . .'

'Oh, yes he *is*.' He checked me in mid-sentence. 'We've already had word from the kidnappers. The silly young sod broke his way out.'

'Silly?' I raised my eyebrows. 'If I was being held that's the one thing . . .'

'Silly,' insisted the big man, 'because his old man was ready and willing to pay. Silly, because he's panicked the kidnappers and put his sister's life at risk. And silly because he now doesn't know who the hell he is.'

'Presumably Lyle knows.'

'No. And he'd better not *get* to know. The slightest whiff of police blue and Mary's life isn't worth a blown-out candle.'

'All Lyle has to do,' I murmured, 'is thumb through a few back copies of *International Construction*, and . . .'

'A publication no working copper is ever without,' he interrupted with a sarcastic edge to his voice.

'It's a risk.' I shrugged. 'I'm trying to earn my salary. Reminding you of the risks.'

'Everything's a risk. Coming to you was a risk.'

'Not at a thousand smackers a day. That's as near to certainty as tomorrow's sunrise.'

'Keep it that way, squire.' The divan seemed to sigh with relief as he stood up. 'We'll be in touch. *I'll* be in touch. No more telephoning. No more anything. You're being retained . . . as from midnight, last night.'

He took a folded cheque from an inside pocket and dropped it onto the divan. It was quite a gesture. The three zeroes after the five made it a particularly *impressive* gesture.

I was still blinking mild disbelief at the cheque as he let himself out.

7.00 p.m.

There are no bad months at Rogate-on-Sands. There are good months and there are not-so-good months. October was one of the not-so-good ones. Not so much for what it was as for what it *promised*. Given the right winds and the right temperature, that old Irish Sea can be as nasty as a wicked step-mother and the wind was veering and the thermometer was falling.

That October evening was an aperitif to the main courses of coming winter.

The anorak kept out the wind other than that which whipped across the front of the hood, but that was enough to make my eyes water. The rising moon gave enough light to see the mackerel sky and what weather lore I knew insisted that *that* meant rain before morning.

That walk along the prom – it had become a habit at

times of indecision. Whenever anything worried me – whenever I needed time to think things out – no matter what the weather, I took the same walk. Past the lifeboat station, past the boating lake, past the pier head then, at the point where the dunes take over, turn round and walk back.

In high season you met people. Out of season and especially in weather like this, you met nobody. It mattered not. I was always alone with my thoughts.

That's what I was doing. Walking and worrying.

The cheque was nice – I was all in favour of the cheque – but what worried me was how the cheque was going to be earned. Nobody gives loot away in slices as thick as *that*. Not to strangers and not without expecting something in return. This Burns Civil Engineering outfit was no hole-in-the-corner building firm. It could afford the best, and that included the best private investigation crowd. Down south, in the Big City, expert negotiators who specialised in dealing with kidnappers were available; the police frowned upon their activities but, more than once, they'd proved their worth and demonstrated their expertise. Therefore, why me and not them? Why pay top price for the Thompson Detective Bureau when the Thompson Detective Bureau was only me, Harry Thompson who, before the big man had dropped the cheque on the divan, had been living on hope and an overdraft?

I had nothing to fall back on. No real experience. Nosing around, with the Fourth Estate playing long-stop, was one thing but playing at go-between with real-life criminals was in a league I'd never before touched.

My thoughts meandered around until, for want of somewhere better to go, they landed on my favourite story-teller. Chandler. I wished Chandler was still alive. More than that, I wished he was walking alongside me on the wind-swept prom of Rogate-on-Sands.

Dear old Phil Marlowe would have known what to do. By this time he would have picked every fly from the ointment and shooed every last wasp away from the honey-pot. He might, of course, have been clobbered, but that was par for the course with any self-respecting American private eye.

It was, it seemed, par for the course with an *English* private eye.

I heard a man's voice softly call my name. I turned to the right and allowed somebody else freedom to clip me above the left ear with something that immediately extinguished the lights.

9.00 p.m.

When the vehicle braked to a halt somebody removed the bandage from my eyes. Nobody removed the surgical tape which kept my wrists fastened behind my back.

I had regained consciousness in the vehicle and, again, the master had been so right. A return to the land of the living, having been hit expertly across the head, brings on an immediate urge to puke. It was an urge I had overcome, but it had been there.

I had awakened in what is technically known as the prone position. Not an uncomfortable position, but one which brought the immediate realisation that the vehicle I was riding in was no ordinary car. I was on some sort of cushioned surface but, when I'd moved a little, I had been warned.

'Lie still, Thompson. You are quite safe.'

Safety, of course, being a very relative thing. Blindfolded, with my hands firmly taped behind my back, in a strange vehicle and not knowing who, or what, my captors were, I had not *felt* safe. On the other hand, I was in no position to argue the point.

Even now, with the blindfold removed, I didn't feel quite *safe*.

I was in one of those home-on-wheels vehicles: a cross between a large van and a caravan. I had been stretched out on one of the side benches. Nobody objected when I swung my feet onto the floor of this miniaturised home.

I thought it wise to make a few mental observations before I became preoccupied with other things. The windows had chintz curtains and the chintz curtains were closed. Illumination came from a remarkably low-powered light in the ceiling. The usual collapsible table had been removed but, beyond an open doorway, I could see the tiny gas-stove and sink. Two men were my immediate captors and they were sitting facing me, on the opposite bench. They were as alike as Tweedledee and Tweedledum: black plimsolls, faded jeans, black high-neck pullovers, black stocking-masks thick enough to hide any hope of recognisable features, black gloves.

Tweedledee held a cosh – presumably the cosh he'd hit me with – and he smacked it rhythmically and gently in the palm of his free hand. It was not an open threat . . . but it left little room for doubt.

Outside, the wind was moving into a higher gear and the van rocked a little with the gusts. We were still on the coast somewhere. I could hear the sea. I could hear the steady pounding of waves but without the hiss of shingle. I decided that we were still near some sort of promenade.

Tweedledum said, 'We understand you are to be Sir Douglas Campbell's emissary.'

It seemed stupid to deny it but dangerous to make any sort of admission. It seemed best to keep a straight face and say nothing.

'We still have Mary,' he said in a steady, almost conversational, tone. 'Alex was a little too clever for us, but we still have Mary. That's all we *really* need. Sir Douglas fully appreciates the situation.'

'What situation?'

It wasn't that I was trying to make things harder for myself. Merely that I wanted this Tweedledum character to keep talking. There had to be a turn of phrase, a twang, a colloquialism – something, anything – that might prove useful. Very few people speak pure and perfect English. This one seemed to be of that few.

'Thompson,' said Tweedledum, 'this is not some sort of guessing game. Sir Douglas would not wish it to be.'

'And you, of course,' I sneered, 'know exactly what Sir Douglas wants and are busting a gut to please him.'

'He wants his daughter back, unharmed.'

'That's all he wants.' I nodded.

'For an agreed sum.'

'Which he's prepared to pay.'

'But *we* must take elementary precautions, of course.'

It was becoming very spooky sitting there in the half-light from the roof bulb, talking civilised talk with a man who was more than a few light years ahead of what the average citizen thinks of when the word 'kidnapper' slips out. This one was both cool and knowledgeable. For starters, he knew *me*. He knew my name. He knew me by sight, otherwise the wrong man might be sitting where I was sitting. Already he knew the connection I had with Campbell and that I was being paid as go-between. He knew a lot too much for my peace of mind.

He even seemed to be able to read my thoughts.

'You were not hard to find, Thompson,' he said.

'I wasn't doing anything to hide myself.'

'Be assured we can find you again, with equal ease, should you deviate in any way from our instructions.'

'*Your* instructions? For what it's worth, my client is Campbell.' I tried a timid smile, and added, 'Unless, of course, you'd like to up the ante.'

'Is that a serious offer?' It was a very deadpan question.

41

'Not really.' I sighed. 'It was a rather weak joke.'

'*We* are not joking, Thompson.'

'No.'

'Sir Douglas Campbell is not jokng.'

'No more jokes,' I promised.

Where the cosh had clipped me my head was beginning to throb a little. There was no heating in the van and the slightly delayed shock of being knocked out was lowering my temperature.

Slowly I was being forced to the conclusion that a thousand a day might *not* be over-generous.

'Okay, no joking,' I growled. 'Where do we go from here? Am *I* kidnapped?'

'No.' The head–mask moved in a gentle negative. 'This has merely been a demonstration. You see, Thompson . . .' He paused, then continued, 'In this type of situation . . .'

'Kidnapping?'

'In this type of situation,' he repeated, patiently, 'we have two choices. If our demands are met, what we require can be delivered by some friend or member of the family, or what we require can be delivered by an acceptable outsider. The friend or member of the family is emotionally involved. This can lead to difficulties which, in turn, can lead to a conclusion with which nobody is satisfied. An outsider is to be preferred. But, even with an outsider, there are certain risks.' Again, he paused for a moment and I had the distinct impression that, behind the mask, he smiled. 'Greed, for example. There is a period when that which is being exchanged is no longer in the hands of the sender but has not yet reached the receiver. There is a temptation.'

'I'm not greedy,' I assured him.

'Not at the moment.'

'Not *ever*. Not *that* greedy.'

'Thompson,' he said, softly, 'everybody has a threshold of greed. Not, perhaps, thirty pieces of silver. But thirty *thousand*? Three *hundred* thousand?'

'You've proved your point,' I said, wearily. 'You can get at me.'

'At any time and wherever you are.'

11.00 p.m.

We took the coast road back to Rogate-on-Sands. It was a quiet drive. The o'clock had seen the drinkers on their way home and the worsening weather kept the joy-riders away from the sea front.

I had been re-blindfolded then helped out of the van and left to fend for myself. The blindfold had been loose enough for me to work it clear of my eyes via a certain amount of contortion with one shoulder. I was charitable enough to believe that the looseness had been deliberate. The tape around my wrists had merely called for more contortion: to lower myself onto my back, bring my knees up to my chin and force my pinioned hands past my backside, clear of my legs and to my front. Thereafter, with the help of my teeth, the surgical plaster had been torn away.

I'd recognised the spot. A car park on the front at Squires Gate – between Blackpool and Lytham St Annes – and little more than twenty miles along the coast, north of Rogate-on-Sands.

I'd found a kiosk, telephoned Liz and now she was returning me to my nest.

She was not too sympathetic.

'You should be kept on a chain,' she said with some irritation. 'Good God! A thousand pounds a day? Even *you* should have smelled rotten fish.'

'I am,' I assured her, 'prepared to tolerate a certain amount of unpleasant odour for that sort of retainer.'

43

'You're a fool.'

'I have a feeling you've expressed that opinion before.'

'Well . . . *aren't* you?'

I let the question hang in the air of the car and hoped that what little concentration she needed to drive would displace her desire to be ill-tempered.

'You're going to report this lot to Lyle, of course,' she said.

'I am *not*.' The contradiction was very emphatic.

'For heaven's sake! These people . . .'

'These people,' I reminded her, 'know what I look like, they know my name and my address and, as they've already demonstrated, they can pick me up – or pick me *off* – whenever they feel it necessary.'

'Damn it, Harry, it's a police matter!'

'Honey . . .' I put my hand on her knee. It was a very innocent gesture. It was not meant to be the first move in a petting session. It was a simple, friendly attempt to emphasise the obvious.

'Stop that!' she snapped.

'Okay.' I spread my palms instead. In a deliberately measured tone, I explained, 'I don't know who the hell they are. I don't know the number of the van . . . assuming it *is* their van. They could be *anybody*. Anybody! That being the case, what can the cops do? What they can't do – what they *won't* do – is give me round-the-clock protection. And even if they could, short of locking me away in some hermetically sealed room, they can't guarantee a thing.' I allowed my mouth the freedom to move into a grin of cynical self-pity. 'I've told you, because I had to tell somebody. Just *somebody*. A thing like this happens and, unless you're Superman, you have to spread it around a little. I'm not Superman. But you, my pet, will keep that kisser of yours very tight-lipped. Because if you *don't* . . .'

I moved a forefinger across my throat.

I needed almost another five miles to convince her that I was not over-reacting.

44

'The Tweedledee character was very eager to do an encore with that cosh. I have bumped into his type before. They *enjoy* hurting people. Given the go-ahead, he'd enjoy taking the first step towards burying me.'

Eventually, she caught on and, having caught on, *she* over-reacted. What could I do? What was I *going* to do? What could *she* do?

I told her what I was going to do. I'd worked out certain obvious angles while waiting at Squires Gate and, when Lytham St Annes was a few miles behind us, I nodded to a parking spot alongside the prom and, without arguing, she pulled in and I explained exactly what *she* had to do.

'Nothing. You do not even mention this trip. I need a sounding board. Somebody to bounce ideas off. That's you, pet. I don't want you part of it, but I want you to know about it. Everything. Then, if things screw up, *then* you can go to Lyle and scream for help.'

Thursday, October 26th

8.00 a.m.

Nobody likes Thursdays. It is too far from one weekend and not near enough to the next. Wet Thursdays, in particular, are a pain in the anus.

This one was a dog. I opened my eyes and, for a moment, thought I was at the thin end of a hangover. Then, I remembered Tweedledee's cosh and the dull ache filling my skull had a better reason. I fingered where the cosh had landed. There was a pigeon-egg-sized lump there and, before swinging my feet from the bed, I toyed with words like 'concussion'.

The hell with 'concussion'. I was on a thousand-a-day salary. If I was ever going to make a name for myself this was the best chance I'd ever have.

The shower steadied me a little and the shave made me feel almost human. As I dressed, the kettle boiled and I sipped scalding instant coffee while tying tie and shoe-laces.

I made a dash through the raindrops and reached the shelter of the car, parked in the yard at the rear of the Wine Bibber, before the soaking reached my skin.

I revved the engine a little, checked the fuel gauge, then pointed the bonnet towards the Pullbury and Norton Rifle and Pistol club.

I was about to break the law, but I didn't much care. When nasty men start bouncing blackjacks from the short hairs behind the ear it is time for dissuasive tactics. Specifically, a loaded Walther semi-automatic pointed in Tweedledee's general direction.

I supposed that, as a last resort, I'd have to shoot the clown. Not kill him. Nothing as drastic as that. I was a good enough shot to send a round into his shoulder or into his thigh. That would immediately cool his ardour. It would also be very illegal.

As I drove I pondered upon the private detectives of the United States. Were they like Phil Marlowe? Were they like Sam Spade? I had gumption enough to doubt it. On the other hand Yankee gun laws did allow responsible citizens the freedom to possess firearms, therefore the American private eye *was* free to carry a gun.

I wasn't! And Liz had blown a sizeable gasket when I'd explained my plan of action.

That didn't matter too much, because Liz was ...

I found myself tooling around with the same old problem. What the hell *was* Liz?

She'd been my wife and, within the strict limits imposed by two people, each determined to pursue a separate career, she'd been a good wife. A *very* good wife. We'd enjoyed the laughs. We'd each willingly offered the other a shoulder to cry upon. For a time – for *most* of the time – we'd gelled.

That was before I cracked. Before the sheer nervous wear and tear of non-stop investigative journalism had smashed me. I'd been like a tree hit by lightning. It had been as sudden and complete as that.

Liz had stuck by me, every miserable inch of the way. She'd taken my irrational rantings – my day after day of whimpering self-pity – and, instead of walking out, had listened to crap and made believe it was sense. She'd soothed and tried to understand. In effect, she'd ironed out the kinks, re-made me . . . *then*, and with the dubious blessing of a shaken man still unable to argue with conviction, she'd walked out.

She had not walked far. To the other side of Rogate-on-Sands where she installed herself in her own flat. That left me with a flat I couldn't afford and a fifty-per-cent share in the cost of an undefended divorce action. It also left me with some pride. I hadn't a job, but nor was I being fed and watered by my wife.

I sold my share of the furniture, moved to rooms above the Wine Bibber and thought up the Thompson Detective Bureau.

And now I was on a thousand-a-day retainer and intended to earn it.

Alfie was one of those men who are born to be a wimp. It wasn't his fault. It was the way he was made. Nevertheless, an accident of birth – *his* birth – didn't mean I had to like him.

He met me as I walked into the 'Pull and Nor' club-room. He was as gushing and as shallow as ever. The smile of welcome stopped at the lips. The greeting contained as much honesty as a broken speak-your-weight machine.

47

He was doing his job, and his job was steward of the club, and I helped pay his wages.

That was the measure of his, 'Harry! It's nice to see you have time enough to make an unexpected visit.'

'I'd like my pistol.'

'Certainly, Harry.' His was the brand of false bonhomie that slipped your first name in every sentence. 'I'll get it for you, Harry.'

I followed him from the club-room. He took the key of the armoury from his pocket. The key was on a ring and the ring was fixed to the belt of his pants via a slim chain.

He said, 'I think there's a range free this afternoon, Harry.'

'It's the firing pin,' I lied.

'Oh!'

'It needs a slight adjustment.'

'Oh.'

Having pointed his nose in the right direction I let things simmer until I had the Walther in my hands.

I checked that it was unloaded, then dry-fired it a couple of times.

'See?' I murmured.

'Well – I – er – I don't know enough about guns, Harry. All I do is . . .'

'It needs a gunsmith,' I insisted. 'It's not something you can do with a screwdriver and a hammer.'

'Oh, I can see that.' He nodded empty wisdom.

'So, if you can find a Disclaimer Form.' I slipped the Walther into my pocket. 'There's a top-class gunsmith at Preston who'll be able to . . .'

'A what?' He stared.

'A gunsmith.'

'No. I mean the form, Harry. I've never heard of . . .'

'A Disclaimer Form. You'll have one in your office, somewhere.'

'I – I can't remember ever having . . .'

'Make it out for fourteen days.' I strolled to the ammo shelves and thumbed eight rounds of 9 mm ammunition from their box. 'It should be back in the armoury before then.'

'Er – fine, Harry. Fine.'

I dropped the ammo into another pocket and, as I turned to leave the armoury, said, 'I'll have a drink before I leave. I'll call in at your office to sign the form . . . if that's okay.'

'Oh sure, Harry. Sure.'

Alfie was an easy man to bluff. Formal technicalities worried him, because he was never *quite* sure. A man with a tiny brain, who didn't want to dirty his hands, the stewardship of the 'Pull and Nor' taxed him to the limit. Any hint of open argument with a member sent him scurrying back to a position of apologetic agreement.

I enjoyed a cider at the bar while Alfie hunted around for a non-existent 'Disclaimer Form'. I wandered into the Stag Section. The copy of *International Construction* wasn't on the table. I fooled myself that Alfie had spotted the torn-out page and removed the magazine.

There was, of course, no 'Disclaimer Form' but Alfie was content when I suggested I write and sign a 'disclaimer' on a sheet of the club's notepaper. He tucked it away in his desk drawer and was happy.

I, in turn, was happy. I had a loaded Walther P.38 waiting for the next time Tweedledee decided to be cosh-happy.

9.00 p.m.

It was still Thursday. The dullest day and the quietest evening of the week. Bull had taken time off to take his grandchildren to see the latest Disney movie at the local cinema.

The Wine Bibber was almost deserted, so I leaned

against the bar, sipped my way through a lonely glass of cider and chatted with Maggie.

Not for the first time, I concluded that Maggie secretly fancied old Bull.

'He's a lovely man to work for,' she said, dreamily.

'If you're kinky for sergeant-majors,' I teased.

'He's a *man*.' She rushed to his defence in overdrive.

'Aren't we all?'

'No . . . not *all*.'

'I sometimes use after-shave,' I admitted with a grin.

'No. Not *you*.' She jerked her head back in a gesture of mild disgust. 'But, some of 'em. Christ! They wear more necklaces and bangles than *I* wear. *And* they drink like tarts.'

That was the level of our conversation. Two people keeping boredom at bay by paddling around in wet words.

I finished my drink, left the bar and discovered I'd been burgled.

The front door latch-lock had been subjected to the celluloid-strip treatment. It had to be celluloid-strip, because there was only one key and I'd just used it. Upstairs a couple of drawers had had their contents emptied onto the carpet and the bedclothes had been pulled back. Somebody had found what they came for. The Walther was no longer under the pillow.

I did not dial 999. It wasn't necessary. I, too, was a 'detective' and the stench of a cheap cheroot still polluted the air of the room.

I dumped the drawer contents back into place and slid the drawers back on their runners. Then I smoked a cigarette and did some weighty planning.

I decided I needed a little back-up knowledge. If possible – which, in effect, meant if he *would* – from Jerry.

I'd worked hand-in-glove with Jerry a few times in the past. He, too, was an IJ. Top flight. He was hard, he was crafty and he worked from a desk at one of the nationals. His was a beat that encompassed international fiddles, armament rake-offs, foreign government back-handers. It could be said he owed me a few favours. The few times he'd ventured north of Watford I'd eased his load a little by providing the opener via which he'd removed the top from some provincial can of worms.

Jerry was in the Super League and I needed either answers or confirmation of certain suspicions. He might be at the office, he might be out of the country, he might be *anywhere* but, if my luck was any good, he'd be at his home.

It was, perhaps, over-reaction but I decided not to use my own telephone. Instead, I called in at the Wine Bibber, changed a note for coins and strolled to the nearest kiosk.

Good fortune had not completely deserted me. After the first few rings, Jerry answered.

I pressed the first coin into the slot and said, 'Jerry? Harry Thompson here. How's life?'

'The crusts still have to be earned.' He sounded to be at ease. He even remembered me. 'Word came through you'd crawled from under.'

'Partly,' I parried. 'I'm still asking awkward questions, but from a different angle.'

'Intriguing.'

'Not really. Private detective work.'

'Ah!'

'That's why I'm ringing.'

'Don't ask *too* much, Harry,' he warned.

'The Burns Civil Engineering Group,' I murmured.

'One of the international outfits.'

'I gathered that much.' With Jerry it was wise to move slowly and with careful deliberation. 'The boss man is Sir Douglas Campbell.'

'As they say,' drawled Jerry, 'if you know, to the

51

nearest million, how much you're worth, you're not *rich*.'

'But he is?'

Where are you speaking from, Harry?'

'A kiosk.'

'A double-check, old friend. I heard the bleeps before you came on.'

'A kiosk,' I repeated.

'For old-time's sake. Don't cross him.'

'Campbell?'

'If it becomes necessary, he'll build a nuclear power plant and send you home through the chimney.'

'As powerful as *that*?' Raised eyebrows went with my question.

'You have my solemn assurance.'

'I'm working *for* him.'

'Correction, Harry . . . you *think* you're working for him.'

'Aren't I?'

'I wouldn't know.' Jerry's quiet chuckle came along the line. 'You'd be surprised how many people have *thought* they were working for him, until he decided otherwise. That gentleman can hire and fire governments . . . and has done, in the past.'

'Big?'

'That's a bit like asking whether Niagara is a waterfall.'

'Oh!'

'Is there anything *I* should know?'

And now Jerry was fishing. He was a pro all the way down to his toe-nails and, as I knew, his was a trade built upon nods, winks and nudges. I spun a mental coin and decided to take one more risk.

'Who's with you?' I asked.

'Nobody.'

'Any likelihood of your phone being tapped?'

'I doubt it. I run a regular check.'

'Are you taping this conversation?'

'Do me a favour?' The indignation sounded genuine.

'Okay.' I nodded at my reflection in the mirror above the kiosk handset. 'Campbell has two kids. Alex and Mary. They've been kidnapped.'

'Sweet Jesus!'

'Alex broke cover. He's on the run. Unfortunately, he's lost his memory and doesn't know who he is.'

'But you know *where* he is?'

'I do.'

'Am *I* to be told where?'

'Not for the moment,' I insisted, gently. 'It might be safer, all round, if he continues *not* to know who he is.'

'Harry, old friend. I need to . . .'

'The story is yours, Jerry,' I promised. 'You have my word it will be an exclusive. But first I need payment. I need as much information as you can give me on Campbell, his family and the Burns Civil Engineering Group. I also need to know something about a man-mountain with whiskers. Name of Dilton-Emmet.'

I still had to tease some of it from him, but not much. What *I* had, plus what I might *eventually* have, was enough to make him sit up and take biscuits.

He told me everything.

He scared the hell out of me.

Friday, October 27th

5.00 a.m.

Having tried to sleep and failed I saw no reason why Alfie should not join me in greeting the dawn. The phone at the 'Pull and Nor' had taken almost five minutes to awaken him and, other than warning him that I was on my way and giving him time to get dressed pending my arrival, I'd told him nothing.

I was going to tell him plenty when I arrived.

I was annoyed, I was pre-dawn tired and my mouth felt as if it had been used as a repository for wet cardboard. The mist which, in places, squeezed itself into patches of fog honed my temper to a fine edge. I tried the car radio but soon grew weary of non-music punctuated by non-conversation. The whole damn world was cold and wet, but nothing was wetter than the clown sitting in the warmth of a radio studio introducing acoustic crap over the air-waves.

There was a light in the club-house and, as I braked on the tarmac apron, the door opened. Alfie had heard me arrive.

He greeted me at the open door.

'Harry. What the . . .'

'Get inside.' I pushed him on the chest and he made a half-step-half-stumble backwards.

I followed him, slammed the door behind me and gave him a second push on the chest.

'Hey, Harry. What the hell . . .'

'A little matter of a Walther,' I snapped. 'A little matter of my place being broken into. And, a little mystery about a magazine that shouldn't have *been* here . . . and now isn't.'

'Look, Harry, I don't want trouble.' He held his hands up, palms forward, as if to push me away. 'I don't want any . . .'

I didn't catch the last word of his sentence. Temporarily, I was deafened. It sounded like a howitzer. It was a .45, but in the enclosed space of the club-room it sounded like a howitzer. The last piece of plaster, from where the bullet had embedded itself in the wall of the club-house, dropped onto the bar-counter as I turned.

'I, on the other hand,' rumbled the big man, 'rather *enjoy* making trouble.'

He was lounging in a chair, in the gloom of one corner. A Walther – *my* Walther – was in his right hand and a Colt .45 revolver grew from his left hand as if it was part of his anatomy. The hint of blue mist was clearing from the muzzle of the .45.

Alfie began sobbing quietly. That's how terrified he was.

The big man grinned and teeth any horse would have been proud of appeared from the undergrowth of whiskers.

'Sit down, Thompson.' He moved the .45 invitingly. Then, to the frightened Alfie, 'A bottle of whisky, some water and two glasses . . . then go for a long walk.'

'I – I – I . . .'

'Do what the nice gentleman says, Alfie.' I threaded a chair between my legs and leaned forward with my folded arms across its back. When Alfie hesitated, I added, 'And, for God's sake, stop sniffling. If he's going to shoot anybody he's going to shoot me.'

'Would I?' Dilton-Emmet showed even more teeth.

'At a guess, you have,' I murmured. 'Many times.'

The big man laughed and Alfie almost ran to the bar, unlocked the grill and produced a still-sealed bottle of Scotch, a glass jug filled with iced-water and two glasses. Neither Dilton-Emmet nor I spoke while Alfie busied himself.

When the whisky, water and glasses were on the table by his elbow, Dilton-Emmet said, 'Fine. Now, take a walk, youngster. Point your nose down the lane, walk for thirty minutes, then turn round and walk back. Understood?'

'Y – yes, sir.'

'You aren't in trouble, Alfie,' I assured him.

'Unless you shorten your walk. In which case, you *are*,' added the big man.

We watched as a worried Alfie worked his way across

the room then almost dived through the door. We continued to wait. Neither of us spoke for more than a full minute.

Then Dilton-Emmet dropped the Walther onto the table, alongside the whisky.

'*That* could cause complications,' he growled.

'To say nothing of Alfie.'

'Alfie?' He looked surprised.

'That one.' I jerked my head towards the door. 'He may be going for a long walk, but he'll be back. Later – when we've both left – he'll scream the place down. He will, my large and hairy friend, crawl from under . . . his kind always do.'

'He won't.' It was a simple statement of fact and, when I raised questioning eyebrows, he added, 'Thompson, we *never* go off at half-cock. One whimper from him – one glance in the wrong direction – and your buddy Lyle will be round. A little matter of sodomy with small boys. It happened a few years ago . . . but insufficient evidence. Lyle will *have* the evidence.'

'Oh!'

'Therefore, we can forget *him*.'

'Every angle.' I sighed.

'Whichever way you turn,' he agreed, cheerfully. 'Thompson, old son, you didn't just "happen". You were *chosen*.' He placed the revolver alongside the Walther and began to unstrip the foil from the neck of the whisky bottle. 'That copy of *International Construction* . . .'

'Don't tell me,' I said, wearily.

'You are a man given to asking questions.' He chuckled. 'You have a natural curiosity. All we did was tune it onto our wavelength.' He unscrewed the top from the bottle, and added, 'How much?'

'Not at this hour.'

'A very civilised man.' He poured a quadruple measure into one of the glasses and, as he added a dash of water,

56

rumbled, 'Me? I tend *not* to be civilised.'

'A very cosy state of mind,' I murmured. Then, 'I'd like my gun back.'

'No way, old son.' He raised the glass and poured almost half of the contents down his throat. 'The first priority is always Campbell's daughter. He'll pay, but he wants her back undamaged.'

'And me?'

'Thompson . . . how to put it?' He raised the glass but, this time, only moistened his lips. 'You are a conduit, my friend. That, and nothing more. The snatch crowd think you're *their* conduit. We *know* you're ours.'

'The "conduit" has already been slightly damaged,' I said. 'The opposition – the snatch crowd, as you call them – have already taken a swing at me.'

'That's understandable.' The information didn't seem to worry him. It wasn't his head that had been blackjacked. 'They have to guard their own backs.'

'What about *my* back?'

'Slightly exposed,' he agreed. The glass made another trip to his mouth. 'But that's what you're being paid for. If it was as easy as you'd *like* it to be we could have used the Royal Mail and saved ourselves money.'

'And – er . . .' I hesitated, then asked, 'If I want out?'

'I doubt if you'd see tomorrow's sunrise,' he said, calmly. 'You already know too much. Far too much. Too much about us and too much about them.'

'A "conduit",' I grumbled, sourly. 'I think a better description would be a nut . . . firmly gripped between the jaws of a nut-cracker.'

'You have a sense of humour, old son.' The whiskers moved as his mouth bowed into a smile. 'You also have a remarkable sense of reality.'

Poets have gone ga-ga about dawn in the open country-side. Homer rattled on about a 'rosy-fingered dawn'.

Milton yapped away about 'the dappled dawn' rising. They are to be congratulated on a vivid imagination.

The only thing that 'rose' on that particular dawn was my own ill-temper. Everything else was cold, wet and gun-metal grey. And the wettest thing around was a certain Harry Thompson who had once figured he could make a modest fortune by shoving his nose into other people's business.

My only consolation was the fact that I'd kept my cool while the hairy monster had demonstrated his control over events. I hadn't done an 'Alfie' . . . although the truth is, I'd been tempted.

On the drive back to Rogate-on-Sands I poked around trying to find some loop-hole in the net the Campbell crowd had dropped over me. I couldn't find one. I doubted if there *was* one. I was the biggest patsy since Jack Ruby had pumped shots into Lee Harvey Oswald.

7.45 a.m.

I left the car, walked round to the door of my hovel, climbed the steps, flicked the gas fire to 'On' then wearily started the rigmarole required for instant coffee. Unlike Dilton-Emmet, my aperitif to a new day was not a king-sized whisky.

I lighted a cigarette and coughed a little while waiting for the water to boil.

I brewed the coffee, took a first tentative sip then heard the first postal delivery of the day arrive.

I ambled slowly back to street level, pending the cooling of the coffee, and tried to guess whether it was the gas bill, the telephone bill or the electricity bill. Other than when

58

asking for money, few people wasted postage stamps on me.

I was wrong. It wasn't a bill. It wasn't even a letter. It was a cigarette-packet-sized parcel. Inside was a key and an unsigned note.

> *Noon today.*
> *Service area north of Junction*
> *No. 15, M6*
> *VW Polo Reg. No. IQP 223.*
> *Instructions in glove*
> *compartment*

The parcel carried a stick-on label with my name, my address and my post-code. Somebody knew more than *I* knew. Whenever I needed my post-code I had to check it out. The parcel had been franked at Rogate-on-Sands the previous day. Just to be sure, the words 'First Class Postage' had been typed top-left of the address.

I did some more detective work upstairs while I drank the coffee.

The *AA Handbook* listed index marks and the registering councils. Nobody issued registration letters IQP. All this proved was that I wasn't the only man in the world who possessed an *AA Handbook*.

All clever stuff!

I dug out a road map and checked the service area north of Junction 15. Not too far from Newcastle under Lyme. Not too far from Stoke-on-Trent.

I figured the journey should top the two-hundred-mile mark and I had to be there for noon. I showered, I shaved, I dressed myself in clean but comfortable clothes, I packed a toothbrush and shaving gear, I checked my cash and credit card, then I was on my way.

I pushed for Preston to get onto the M6 and, somewhere along the way, I saw the car behind me. It was a Merc, it could have shown me a clean pair of heels but it didn't, even though the roads were clear and there was no local speed restriction. In such circumstances a nasty, suspicious mind seemed appropriate.

I allowed the Merc at easy tail until we reached Preston, then I pulled a gag as old as the hills but a gag which never fails.

Preston (as I knew) is a town with an abundance of traffic lights. I nipped smartly in front of a lorry and headed away from the M6 lead-in roads. I made damn sure the lorry was too close to my rear to allow the Merc to tuck itself between us, then I watched the traffic lights as we approached them. I found one at green – one that had been at green for some time – then slowed slightly and, as the lights changed, gunned the car and hit the crossroads fractionally against the lights. In the mirror I saw the lorry brake to a halt at the red and, behind the lorry, the Merc had no choice.

I turned left, then left again, then weaved a way through back streets until I was back, facing the M6. I gave myself a ten-minute zig-zag course, then parked on the forecourt of a hole-in-the-corner filling station with the excuse that I needed to use the men's room.

When I returned to the car I was happy.

I'd lost the Merc.

Noon

I'd tried to hit it as near to the button as possible, but without being late. I'd killed a little time at the Sandbach Service Area a few miles back, called Liz to warn her I might be away for some time, then sipped motorway tea. The object was to be neither late nor early.

I pulled onto the slip-road and turned onto the parking area as the sweep hand on the dashboard clock nibbled away the last few seconds to midday.

I saw the VW. It didn't look new. It didn't look old. It was dark blue and it looked very ordinary. The number-plates were yellow and read IQP 223. Maybe the number-plates looked a little newer than the car. I thought they did ... but perhaps only because they *had* to be.

I found a quiet corner of the parking area, parked my own jalopy, locked the doors and pocketed the keys. Despite the time of year a fair number of people were strolling to and from cars and a man in a peaked cap seemed to be keeping a lazy eye on things.

It seemed prudent not to make directly from one car to the other. I wandered into the self-service restaurant, bought myself a ham sandwich and more motorway tea, then found a table near a window from where I could watch the VW.

I finished the ham sandwich, lighted a cigarette, fiddled around with the key I'd been sent and felt both scared and guilty.

I think I'd watched too many TV cops-and-robbers episodes. I found myself toying with the possibility that the VW might explode when I turned on the ignition.

I was (I told myself) quite crazy.

Having decided I was crazy, I took a deep breath, left the restaurant and acted as if I *owned* the VW.

The key was the usual thing. Door-lock/ignition. I settled into the driving seat then leaned sideways and opened the glove compartment. There was an envelope and, inside the envelope, there was another unsigned note.

> *South to Junction No. 12*
> *East on the A5*
> *Dinner, bed and breakfast*
> *at the King's Head, Aylesbury*

I shrugged. It was one way of seeing parts of the country I'd never seen before.

I think I closed my eyes as I turned the key in the

61

ignition, but the engine gunned into immediate life . . .
and that was all.

4.00 p.m.

Having unwound myself from a demonic one-way-street
system thought up by the top citizens of Aylesbury I
threaded the VW through the entry tunnel leading to the
cobbled yard of the King's Head.

I am no history buff, but even *I* was rather taken with
this fifteenth-century hostelry. The courtyard in which I
parked the VW was made for stage-coaches. The clatter
of hoofs and the rattle of harness were the true sounds for
such surroundings.

At the reception desk the proprietor gave me the
welcoming patter.

'Ah yes, Mr Thompson. You're booked in. Dinner,
bed and breakfast.'

'Everything paid for?' It was a question I'd been waiting
to ask.

'Of course.' He looked surprised.

'Of course.' I nodded and signed the register. As
off-handedly as I could make it, I said, 'Who by?'

'Sir?'

'Who's footing the bill for my stay here?'

'Burns Civil Engineering, of course. I thought you'd . . .'

'Of course.'

I smiled a smile which I knew was forced. The proprietor was looking a mite suspicious. The socking great
Alsatian which seemed to be his companion-cum-minder
was eyeing me warily.

I said, 'I need pyjamas. I – er – there's been some slight
misunderstanding. When I set off I didn't expect to spend
the night away from home.'

'The shops in the square will still be open.'

'Thank you.'

'Your table's booked for eight o'clock.'

'Fine. Fine.'

I was being manipulated. Friend, was I being manipulated! I was being told where to go and *when* to go. I
was being told when to arrive. Where to sleep and, now,
when to eat. I was being made to look something of a
lemon . . . and I didn't know who was squeezing me.

Thus the annoying thoughts as I wandered around
Aylesbury shopping centre. I bought myself pyjamas. I
also bought myself a mac and a new shirt. I found a sports
outfitters and bought myself a knife. A hunting knife, with
a six-inch blade and a good sheath. Having bought the
knife, I strolled around until I found a shop which sold
me a leather belt.

I strolled back to the hotel and up to my room. A
brew-it-yourself kit was there for use and I sipped even
worse-than-usual instant coffee as I smoked cigarettes and
watched the screen of the bedroom's TV set. What I was
watching didn't register. It could have been paint-stripper
at work for all I knew.

I was thinking.

Very slowly the cogs were going round.

7.30 p.m.

I had bathed and run a razor across my face to freshen
up a little. I was now dressing and tooling around with
the hunting knife and the belt.

It is no exaggeration to say I felt a little foolish. Here I
was in the bedroom of a very civilised Olde Worlde hotel,
little more than twenty miles from London, and tarting
myself up like a latter-day Davy Crockett.

I hoped, most earnestly, that that was all I *was* doing.
That I wouldn't have to *use* the knife. Nevertheless by this

time the penny had dropped. I was caught up between two organisations, both of which had money. Money with noughts disappearing into the middle distance. Both ruthless. Both capable of high-bidding some homicidal bastard into creeping up on me and making damn sure my life lasted only as long as my usefulness.

The Walther would have given comfort. The hairy monster had denied me the use of the Walther, therefore all I had left was the hunting knife.

I fixed it under my shirt. I used the belt I'd bought. It took a certain amount of manoeuvring but, eventually, I had what amounted to a high cross-draw, with the hilt of the knife about six inches below my left armpit and the sheathed blade down my left side. It wasn't too much in the way and if I left a button of my shirt undone it was fairly easily get-at-able.

I felt a bit of a prat as I walked down to the dining room . . . but I also felt a little more easy in my mind.

8.00 p.m.

The panelled dining room was very atmospheric. A place of polished wood and leaded windows. A place that could have been gloomy, but wasn't. Nothing chrome and plastic here. Just good timber, fine linen and gleaming cutlery. Henry VIII would have felt at home.

The waitress led me to a table and I ordered a fruit drink for starters, followed by Aylesbury duck with all the trimmings. It seemed only appropriate.

My companion at the table had already ordered. His, it turned out, was the traditional roast-beef-Yorkshire-pudding choice. That, too, seemed appropriate.

I glanced around the room as I waited. It wasn't full, but neither was it empty. Maybe ten – maybe a dozen – other people were eating. At a guess, most of them were

64

locals having a meal out. Nobody was within easy hearing distance of us.

The first course arrived. My table companion had ordered soup.

We smiled at each other. Each gave that tiny nod which the Englishman gives to acknowledge that he is not the sole occupant of a room, or indeed of the world.

I mentally classified him as Afro-Asian. His skin matched the dark wood of the panels, but his features were too finely chiselled for a full-blooded native of the Dark Continent. His jet hair was straight and parted and expertly barbered. He wore a white shirt, a grey tie and a charcoal-coloured suit whose cut made my clothes seem like rejects from Oxfam.

He finished his soup. I finished my fruit juice. The waitress cleared the first course and delivered the main part of the meal.

'Are you a good man, Mr Thompson?'

The question was asked in gentle, precisely spoken words. I looked up and saw my companion smiling at me. I envied him his perfect teeth.

'Forgive me for asking,' he murmured.

'Tweedledum.' I breathed.

'I beg your pardon?' The smile remained and did not become fixed.

'The last time we met,' I said, softly, 'your buddy had just coshed me.'

'Not too hard, I think.'

'Hard enough,' I assured him. Then, 'Tell me, friend – friend Tweedledum – what's to stop me from walking to the nearest phone . . .'

'Ringing for the police?' The mockery was very polite.

'Just that.' I nodded, then continued teasing pieces of duck from the carcass.

'You won't do that, Mr Thompson.' He, too, continued his meal as we talked. It was all very civilised. 'Sir Douglas

65

is not paying you to *involve* the police. He is paying you to keep the police *out* of this situation.'

'That same old word,' I remarked pleasantly.

'Which word is that?'

'"Situation." You used it the last time we talked.'

We ate in companionable silence for a few moments before he spoke again.

'You haven't answered my question, Mr Thompson.'

'What question was that?'

'Are you a good man?'

Before I could answer, the wine waiter arrived. I'd ordered a modest, supermarket white but, nevertheless, we had to wait until the empty ritual of tasting, nodding and having it poured had been gone through and the waiter had left the table.

'I am *not* a good man.' I moistened my lips with wine before I continued, 'For what it's worth – and bearing in mind my profession before I took up this lark – I don't think the genuinely *good* man exists. Some of us are better than others. if you press the point, I'd describe myself as "average".'

'Could you kill?'

'Oh, yes.' I chewed as I gave a slow, nodding affirmative. 'I could kill. I hold the opinion that everybody could kill – quite happily *would* kill – given certain circumstances.'

'For money?'

'That depends how *much* money . . . and who I'd be expected to kill.'

'I find you a refreshingly honest man, Mr Thompson.' He smiled.

'There's less hassle that way,' I assured him.

Again there was a silence while we chewed and swallowed. This time it was a slightly prolonged silence.

He said, 'I was educated in your country, Mr Thompson.'

'Not born here.'

66

'No . . . not born here.'

'That accounts for it.'

'What?'

'A lack of regional dialect. Very few Englishmen pronounce their words as perfectly as you do.'

'I was born,' he said, 'in a country which, these days, would be described as "backward". One of the so-called "emergent nations" being hauled, struggling, into the twentieth century.'

'They shouldn't struggle,' I remarked. 'It's a better century than most.'

'We don't think so,' he contradicted, gently. 'Ours was a tribal community. A nomadic community of hunters who fed themselves and their flocks on what nature provided in abundance. We had no cities. No central government. We were simple, but happy.'

I looked across the table at him, smiled and remarked, '*You* don't give the impression of a man with too many worries.'

'I have been "Westernised".' The words were tightly spoken and carried a peculiar shame. 'My priorities have been made untrue. For a time – for a *long* time – I considered myself lucky.'

'But a "good" man?' And if my question was touched with mockery it was meant to be gentle mockery.

We once more ate in silence and, this time, the silence stretched until I was quite sure I'd offended the man. He was a coloured man and, quite possibly, touchy. Despite his very obvious Western education, the chances were that he hadn't – and never *could* have – assimilated the custom of giving and receiving mild leg-pulling as part of normal conversation.

Not that it worried me unduly. The man was a kidnapper or, at the very least, part of a kidnapping organisation. For me, and however smooth his manner, he was as bent as a crummock. I'd seen far too many smarm merchants in the past to be conned by this one.

At last he said, 'Mr Thompson, imagine an area about the size, say, of Wales. Good grazing land. A certain amount of bush in which animals capable of being killed for food live and have their environment. The whole area surrounded by mountains. Mountains which, in a season you might call winter, are inhospitable other than on their lowest slopes. Mountains which – winter *or* summer – give little or no grazing.'

I glanced up to let him know I was listening, but continued eating and listening.

'There are rivers,' he continued. 'There is one particular river. Like an artery. It flows through this land – through that *good* part of this land – and it provides water for both men and animals.' He paused to load his fork then, before he transferred the food to his mouth, he went on, 'To dam this river at a certain point – at a point already surveyed – would provide electricity. Enough electricity to light up a capital city. The capital city of this land of which I speak, but a capital city well away from the rich land of the plain and beyond the ring of mountains.'

He chewed while I visualised what his words meant. I was *meant* to visualise, and I was meant to be shocked, but I wasn't.

'The artificial lake, created by the building of this dam,' he moved his fork to emphasise his words, 'will cover the good land, of course. The pasture. It will rob my people of land upon which they have always lived. They will starve. They will die.'

'Talking of dying,' I murmured, 'what will happen to his daughter if Sir Douglas Campbell doesn't pay the ransom?'

'He will pay.' He sounded very certain.

'I'm inclined to agree.' I sipped wine. 'And, while we're discussing dams ... the Burns Civil Engineering Group, perhaps?'

'You are a very perceptive man, Mr Thompson.'

'No. Just not dumb ... and, by your yardstick, not "good".'

He cocked his head, enquiringly.

Still in a pleasant enough voice, I said, 'When a creep who's part of a snatch racket starts asking *me* if I'm "good" I get to thinking "up" is suddenly down there somewhere and "down" is higher than the clouds. We are arse-about-face with each other, friend. We are talking opposites.' This time *I* used my fork to point. 'That beef you're eating. Good English beef from a cow reared in comparative luxury. Milked via electricity. Probably fed via electricity. Killed humanely. Its meat kept fit to eat via electricity. And now you're noshing it surrounded by everything electricity can offer. From where you're sitting, friend, you can *afford* to preach a back-to-nature sermon. Go live in a tent for a couple of years ... *then* tell me.' I leaned forward slightly and ended, 'One more thing. Your pal with the cosh. Give him due notice. If I ever get as near to *him* as I am to *you*, he won't have to ask. He'll know damn well that, by *his* measuring rod, I'm not a "good" man ... he'll know that while he's picking the teeth from the back of his throat.'

It was hard talk. I knew it was the brand of talk which might, eventually, bring me physical pain. I didn't give a damn. It was the mood I was in, and the mood was resultant upon my having been made something of a patsy.

I need hardly say we ended our meal in frost-edged silence.

11.45 p.m.

I settled down to sleep.

I'd done what I could to ensure I would not be disturbed.

I had locked the bedroom door but, because there are

such things as pass keys, I had wedged a chair with its back hard under the knob of the door. I had taken a wire coat-hanger from the wardrobe and ruined it by twisting it around the two levers of the cockspur fasteners which held the windows closed. I had arranged for a 6.30 a.m. call. I had the unsheathed hunting knife to hand, under the pillow.

I was ready for just about anything.

Nothing happened.

Saturday, October 28th

7.30 a.m.

The streets had that cold, pre-dawn gloom, but I needed the air and the exercise. The occasional London-bound commuter gunned the cold engine of his car through the near-deserted market square and sent purple fumes from its exhaust. One prize prat heading full-throttle for a heart attack flat-footed past me in the full jogging gear. A couple of elderly gents were taking their dogs for the first walk of the day. A lonely copper sauntered past the still-closed shops and glanced at their doors with bored disinterest.

That was the sort of world it was and, for as long as it took me to smoke a pre-breakfast cigarette, I joined it.

Tweedledum did not join me in the dining room. Nobody joined me in the dining room. Maybe I was the only guest. It was possible. It was an odd time of the year. Come to that, maybe Tweedledum hadn't been a guest. Maybe he'd just called in for dinner and to check that the puppet was behaving correctly.

If so, it made all the hunting-knife palaver look a little stupid.

I didn't give too much of a damn. I had kippers, followed by toast, marmalade and coffee and saw no reason to rush things. I enjoyed my second cigarette of the day, collected what little luggage I had and returned to the VW.

This time the note read:

> *North on the A5.*
> *North on the M1.*
> *Service area north of*
> *Junction No. 38 at 4.30 p.m.*

The envelope containing the note was on the driving seat.

I sighed, hoiked my gear onto the rear seat and sadly concluded that the puppet had little choice *but* to behave correctly. I was obviously being made to do a yo-yo act up and down the motorway system and I wondered how many more times I would be made to criss-cross this not-so-green and distinctly unpleasant land. Was I being watched and timed? What the hell would happen supposing the car went on the blink? So many 'ifs' and so many 'buts', and all I could do was read unsigned billets-doux and hope whichever bed was waiting for me would be moderately comfortable.

I settled behind the wheel, groped my way out of the town Anne Boleyn's old man once favoured and pointed the nose of the VW towards the A5.

Somewhere on the A5 I pulled onto the forecourt of a decent-looking café. I ordered a cheese sandwich and tea while I used the pay phone to call Liz at her office. I gave her the number of the phone I was using and asked her to call back from a public kiosk.

I was being very careful. Bugged or not, the firm Liz

worked for had a switchboard manned by bored females. I couldn't even take *that* much of a chance.

I'd just about gagged my way through soggy bread and mousetrap cheese when the café telephone rang and, having answered it, the biddy from behind the counter called me over.

'What on earth are you up to?' Liz sounded very scratchy.

'Up to the eye-balls,' I said, grimly.

'Where are you speaking from?'

I told her, then added, 'At half-four, this afternoon, I'm due at a service area on the M1. North of Junction Thirty-eight.'

'And?'

'For Christ's sake!' I held my mouth close to the phone. 'Liz, I'm being made a monkey of, and I don't know how to get from under.'

'It's easy. Just walk away.'

'Don't be so damned stupid, woman. They know where I *live*, they know I use the "Pull and Nor", they know I walk along the prom fairly regularly. They have me neat and tidy in pink ribbon.'

'If you call me "woman" again,' she threatened, 'this receiver goes back on its rest.'

'I'm sorry, pet . . . I'm sorry.' Panic was in there, because I felt panic. I gabbled, 'Liz, my love, I'm in a muck sweat. They have me lined up. For *anything*. And I don't know who they are or where they are. I need back-up.'

'From me?'

'From Jerry. You know Jerry, the chap who . . .'

'I know Jerry,' she interrupted.

'Contact him.' I gave her Jerry's home number and office number. 'Tell him about the appointment at the service area.' I gave her the registration number of the VW. 'Tell him I need him. Tell him it's big . . . and it's all his.'

'Is that wise?' She sounded doubtful.

'Liz. *Please!* Find him and tell him. He knows enough already. He'll take off and he can damn near *push* a car there by half-past four.'

'If you're quite sure.'

'I'm sure. I'm *sure.*'

She wished me luck and I thanked her, then I rang off and returned to what was left of the cheese sandwich and tea. I'd done what I could, and all I could. Whoever was organising this merry-go-round had dropped his first clanger. He'd allowed the schedule to slacken enough for me to introduce my own reinforcements. An earlier time at the service area and Jerry wouldn't have been able to make it. But 4.30 p.m. – given the fast lane of a motorway starting at Hendon and the way Jerry drove his Aston Martin – and he'd be there before I was.

People say there is no north/south divide. People say crazy things all the time. Most people who disclaim this division live south of Luton Airport, and maybe they believe it, but they are wrong.

Bang up the M1, my friend, and watch what happens north of Rugby. Gradually – very gradually at first – the foliage and the grass change colour. There is less lushness and the autumn tints of the south take on a uniform yellow. There is a dankness; an odd feeling of oppression, as if the smoke and muck of the Black Country are acclimatising the traveller to the heavier grime of the Industrial North.

On the other hand, maybe I was kidding myself. Maybe I was wearying of sitting behind the wheel of a car which wasn't my own. Maybe there only *seemed* to be more clapped-out lorries and vans using the motorway as I drove north.

By Junction 22 I was ready for a break. I was tired of motorway driving. I had all the time in the world. I knew a fine eating spot at Ashby de la Zouch, so I

73

swung west on the A50 and made for Market Street and the Ashbeian.

I dawdled over the meal. I strolled the streets for a while. There was a possibility I was being watched. I was almost sure I wasn't . . . but only *almost* sure. My dinner companion at the King's Head had removed any conviction of absolute certainty.

I wanted to give Jerry time enough to arrive before I did. I knew Jerry. I knew how he worked. He'd check the cars already there, then he'd find some position where he could watch every car arrive.

That's what I wanted.

If he saw me arrive he'd keep his eyes skinned for anybody else watching for me to arrive. With luck, and between us, we might be able to jump a move and get ahead.

4.30 p.m.

The old 'greasy spoon' image of motorway cafés has been improved of late, but the architecture remains the same. 'Slot-machine Arcade' style with an overlay of 'Public Toilet'. They are dreary places and they cater for travellers inescapably trapped within the elongated prison which links one junction with the next. They allow weary limbs to rest and cramped muscles to stretch themselves. Of necessity, much of their area is parking space but, at that time of the day and at that season of the year, most of the parking space is unoccupied.

I drove slowly into the parking lot and I drove the long way round. I spotted the Aston Martin. It wasn't difficult. It is not too common a make of car. It was empty, and I braked the VW into a vacant space less than ten yards from where it was parked.

Jerry was around. It gave me a warm and comfortable

feeling. Jerry, I was sure, would have seen me. I refrained from deliberately looking for him. I made believe I was alone, locked the VW, strolled into the toilets and, from there, went into the self-service restaurant.

I bought tea, smoked a cigarette and waited.

I waited for almost an hour and nothing happened. It was quite dark outside and I began worrying.

I decided I ought, perhaps, to have stayed with the VW. I hurried back to where I'd parked it. It was still there. It was still empty.

A voice said, 'To the lorry park, please, Mr Thompson.' I began to turn and the voice continued, 'Don't! Just walk quietly to the lorry park.'

I shrugged and obeyed orders.

The heavy goods vehicles were parked in neat ranks. High-sided vehicles with canyons of darkness between each pair.

The voice said, 'Turn right, Mr Thompson,' and I did.

It was eerie. The darkness was just about complete in the narrow space between the tarpaulined loads. The noise from the entrance hall of the restaurant was cut off completely.

'You may look round, now.'

I did and, before I saw the man, I saw the folded newspaper b. 'ng removed from the silencered snout of the pistol.

'No one would ever know,' warned the man, and I believed him.

As he let the newspaper fall to the ground he said, 'Now keep walking, Mr Thompson. Slowly. Try not to do anything foolish.' A pinpointed light from a torch danced ahead of me for a moment, and he added, 'If you *need* proof of how serious we are . . .'

The tiny light illuminated Jerry's face for a moment. He was there, sprawling in a rag-doll awkwardness, half-hidden beneath the towering bulk of an articulated vehicle.

His eyes were still open, but he'd see nothing again. The bullet-hole at the root of his nose was almost geometrically positioned. A black hole, but not much blood. The blood – a lot of blood – came from the exit hole at the rear of his skull.

I could see the man more plainly when he switched on the lights inside the furniture van.

It *was* a furniture van. A particularly large furniture van, with a door at the side through which he had pushed me. Externally, it *was* a furniture van. Internally, it was a remarkably well-furnished prison.

The man had wasted no time. Before switching on the lights – before sliding the bolts which double-secured the door through which we'd entered – he'd grasped one of my wrists and clamped a handcuff into place. *Then* he'd switched on the lights and pressed a bell-push let into the wall of the prison.

I looked at the man with the silencered pistol. I noted him well, because I wanted to remember him for the rest of my life. Or *his* life. Or until I saw him being escorted from some Crown Court dock having been convicted of murdering Jerry.

Not Tweedledum.

But from the same matrix. Brown skin and Asian-featured. Neatly cut hair but, this time, with a touch of grey at the wings. Dark, intelligent eyes. Sneakers, good class, khaki twill trousers, an expensive wind-cheater, collar and tie. The bearing – his manner of quiet, educated ruthlessness – the soul-deep fanaticism which he did little to hide. He was on a par with Tweedledum. At a guess, more dangerous than Tweedledum.

'My apologies, Mr Thompson.' There was a distinct sneer in the tone. 'We must be sure at all times ... obviously.'

'The regal pronoun.' I tried to match him, tone for tone,

although it took no small effort to control my voice. 'Just exactly what are you king *of*?'

'Of this little world.' He allowed me full view of the pistol before he placed it on a shelf, well beyond my reach.

'You killed my friend.' I made it a flat, no-nonsense statement.

'I killed a man who might have become my enemy,' he contradicted, quietly.

'That makes *me* your enemy.'

'Not yet.' A tight smile came and went. 'Be advised, Mr Thompson. Hope you never *become* my enemy.'

The girl chipped in with, 'He doesn't know what they're trying to do, Hanji. When he knows, he'll understand. They aren't *all* like my father.'

'Hanji?' I cocked a quizzical eyebrow. 'A nice Moslem name.'

'Perhaps.'

'Mohammed would be proud to know you, Hanji.' I didn't give a damn which religion he followed. I was out to needle him. 'A murderer of unarmed men. A kidnapper of little girls.'

'I'm not a "little girl",' she almost shouted the words at me. 'And I'm not "kidnapped" . . . at least, not now.'

'A soiler of minds,' I mocked. 'A corrupter of children.'

'I'm not a child. *I'm not a child!*' Then, in a hysterical scream, 'Kill him, Hanji. He'll never understand. He's one of *them. Kill him* . . . before it's too late.'

11.30 p.m.

The bunk bed was comfortable enough and I'd done what I'd set out to do. I'd needled the Hanji character enough to make him forget certain basics.

The lunatic female had helped, of course. Nothing

77

would have given her greater pleasure than to have torn my heart out with her bare hands. For fifteen minutes (thereabouts) all hell had been let loose in that furniture van as it trundled its way towards wherever it was going. Hanji had kept enough of his cool to remember that I was something more than a pretty face. I was the guy who would, eventually, deliver the loot. That being the case, I had to be kept upright and in working order. The girl (Mary Campbell, as ever was!) didn't give a damn about money. She wouldn't, of course ... when you own a whole forest you don't concern yourself with the odd twig!

Hanji had slapped her. A good, old-fashioned, Moslem belt across the chops. And that *had* quietened her.

'Control yourself, girl. For the moment, you are a means to an end. Do not forget that, otherwise you will become a mere nuisance.'

Then, to me, 'Thompson, you are not indispensable.'

'Don't bet on it, Hanji, my boy,' I'd murmured.

'You are *not* indispensable.' I think he'd been trying to convince himself. He hadn't quite convinced me. 'Behave in a civilised manner. Use the bed, and remember ...'

'I know. I'm not indispensable.'

He'd given harsh words of warning to the girl before collecting the pistol and leaving through a door in the front of the prison arrangement. Presumably to join others in the cab of the vehicle.

Which was very nice. A kerfuffle. A couple of lost tempers. And I still had the hunting knife under my shirt.

Harry Thompson. Private detective and smart-aleck.

But Jerry was dead, which meant the goal posts had been moved and the rules of the game had been changed. Things had suddenly become very personal.

Jerry had not been my bosom pal. Nothing like that. Just that I'd liked him, trusted him and that we'd once worked rather well together. I'd asked him for a favour and he'd obliged. Okay, he was sniffing out a story and that might have been the real reason for him being at the service area, but I was the one who'd hinted at a possible scoop, therefore I was also the reason for him being there. And now the only scoop going would be based upon *his* murdered corpse.

I allowed myself to ride with the roll of the van and thought a lot. I wondered why the hell I wasn't scared witless, and decided I *was*. But I was also angry. Bloody angry! And the anger swamped the fear and made it unimportant.

As for the girl . . .

This one was a collector's item. She wore a white jump suit and pumps. Her hair was fixed in that throw-away, slightly untidy style that costs the earth. She was about sixteen – maybe seventeen – which meant she already knew everything and was far too wise and experienced to take advice.

She was a pain. However much her father was paying for her return, he was being gypped.

She stared her hatred at me from the bunk bed upon which she sprawled. She was no more comfortable and no less comfortable than I – the handcuff was attached to a thin chain and the chain ended in a ring which, in turn, circled a rod running the length of *my* bunk bed – but, whereas I had spent the journey with my thoughts, *she* had concentrated upon giving me some sort of evil-eye treatment.

I turned to face her across the van. That stupid moon-like face, with the slobbering lips and the spoiled arrogance of the eyes. Some ridiculous school – a very expensive school, no doubt – had taken a normal child and force-fed that child far too much stupidity for its own good.

'You seem to approve of what these people are doing to your father,' I said.

She merely glared a darker hatred across the few feet which separated us.

'Don't you?' I insisted.

'You don't know what you're talking about,' she spat.

'But you *do*?'

'I know what *he*'s doing to *them*.'

'From what I can gather, he's building them a dam.'

'You're a fool. You don't know how big a fool you *are*.'

'He's *not* building them a dam?'

'Of course he is.'

'In that case, I can't see . . .'

'But that's not all he's doing. He's deliberately depriving them of their livelihood. He's starving them to death.'

'Them?' I motioned with my head to where friend Hanji had disappeared. 'Those creeps?'

'Their fellow-countrymen. Their . . .'

'You stupid little bitch.' I chose my words and spoke them deliberately. 'All this hot-shot gospel about flooding the grazing pastures of some moth-eaten tribes. You really think Hanji and his buddies give a monkey's toss about their wandering brethren? No way! Forget nationality, my crazy little moralising cow. These boys – the bunch who, whether you like it or not, *have* kidnapped you – believe in the stuff that's made your life easy. They are educated. They are also bent. They wouldn't know how to milk a cow if they had one, and they've never slept in a tent in their lives.'

'You don't know what you're talking about.'

She'd said it before but, this time, she didn't quite mean it. Oh, she wasn't wrong – her kind are never *wrong* . . . but, given enough obvious proof, they can handle being ever so slightly mistaken.

'They're also murderers,' I said calmly.

'That's a lie for a start. They haven't laid a hand on me, and I've been . . .'

'Other people live in this world.' My interruption

80

smacked her into silence. I allowed my disgust to ride what I was saying. 'Not just you, young lady. Not just the people *you* see fit to recognise. People who have a right to live. The right to die in their own time and in their own place.

'A chap called Jerry. A friend. *My* friend. He was around at our last stopping place. He was there to help me . . . indirectly to help *you*. That Hanji bastard didn't know him, but that didn't stop him from using that silencered gun of his. Right between the eyes, fair maiden. Where, no doubt, you wanted him to shoot me.'

'I – I didn't mean . . .'

'We've left him there, in a car park. He just happened to be in the way. A hindrance. No more. So they swotted the poor sod, much as they might swot an annoying insect. But he wasn't an insect. He was a man. A good man, and my friend. *That* is the company you're keeping . . . and you're crazy enough to believe the crap they're feeding you about the brotherhood of man.'

'I don't believe you,' she breathed.

'It doesn't matter.' I took the packet from my pocket and lighted a cigarette. 'What you believe – what you disbelieve – put them both together and they don't add up to a gnat's fart. I know the truth. And the truth is that, short of him killing *me*, I'm going to drop your friend Hanji-boy in a dock, facing a charge of murder. *Then* he'll have something more important on his mind than other people's tents.'

Sunday, October 29th

1.45 a.m.

'Did he *really* murder your friend?'

I had been dozing. Not quite asleep but in that nice

81

halfway state where the mind is dawdling around a dreamy landscape of might-have-beens dotted with sad little wisdoms-after-the-event. Not dreams . . . rather realities which had been missed.

I blinked into full wakening and turned my head.

'Your friend,' she repeated. 'Did Hanji *really* murder him?'

'He did,' I answered, shortly.

'I didn't think he would,' she said, solemnly. 'I didn't think he was that sort of man.'

'Child.' I tried to be as patient as I could. 'He is a kidnapper. That, at least, you have proof of. It's not too far from that to the other thing.'

'Nobody's ill-treated me.' I think she was trying to justify her previous contentions. 'They could have.'

'They bounced your brother around a little,' I grunted.

'My brother?'

'Alex . . . what the hell his name is. Before *he* broke loose, they . . .'

'Have they kidnapped *Alex*?'

This time it was my turn to stare.

'Have they?' she demanded, and there was urgency in her tone. 'Have they kidnapped Alex, as well as me?'

'He broke free,' I said in order to give myself time to take things in. Then I asked, 'Didn't you know? That they'd kidnapped you *and* Alex?'

'No. Of course not. How could I know a thing like . . .'

'Both at the same time,' I grunted.

'What?'

'That's what I took to have happened. That they picked you both up at the same time.'

'Don't be so stupid.' She was back to being stroppy again.

'Okay.' I swung my feet from the bunk bed and faced her. 'Tell me where I'm stupid.'

'Not both at the same *time*. You don't know us. You don't know our family. Alex and I – we like each other well enough – but we were never *with* each other. We don't even live in the same house. I live with Father and have a flat in London. Alex lives with his girl-friend just along the coast from Dundee. A place called Monifieth. I've never been there, but . . .'

That's how it started. That's how we talked. We did not become 'friends' – she was far too stupid a little cow for me ever to sully a perfectly good word by calling her *that* – but we came to acknowledge our mutual existence. I was being paid to acknowledge her. Very gradually she was becoming scared enough to *want* to acknowledge somebody. Somebody who just *might* be able to pluck her from the fertiliser she'd surrounded herself with.

'I believed them, Mr Thompson. I *honestly* believed them. I'm still not *quite* sure, one way or the other.'

'Kiddo, we may not be sharing the same bed, but we're near enough for you to start calling me "Harry".'

'All right . . . Harry. I don't know *what* to believe.'

'Play it safe. Don't believe anybody.'

It was good advice. Whether she took it or not, I didn't know. The chances were she didn't. Her life-style had made her contemptuous of advice. What she didn't know wasn't *worth* knowing.

Nevertheless, and in her own way, she talked.

The price on her head was a cool million. Tweedledee – Hanji – what the hell his name was, had told her that much. One million pounds, sterling, in used ten, twenty Bank of England notes. That plus a cancellation of the contract to build the infernal dam.

I didn't believe the cancellation of the dam part. That was pure tinsel, meant to give the deal an air of pseudo-respectability. Old man Campbell might be able to rustle up the seven-figure ransom but, sure as hell, he couldn't walk away from a contract to provide a government with a dam. The home address of *that* little number was well inside Cloud–cuckoo–Land.

'Pop should be able to pay the million.' She made it sound like the entrance fee to a football match.

'Great. That should pay for fish and chips all round.'

2.30 a.m.

Hanji was definitely Tweedledee . . . but *definitely*!

His skill with a blackjack removed any doubts. Same spot. Same amount of energy. Same unexpectedness.

I'd heard the door to the front of the van open and, without immediately looking, I'd hoisted myself onto an elbow and caught a fleeting glimpse of white teeth in a brown face. No more. At that point the cosh had landed and the curtains had been closed.

And now I was alone, in a country lane, trying to keep my stomach in place and holding the spot behind my ear which, for the second time, had taken a belting.

It was cold and I felt strangely naked. I checked and pinpointed the feeling of nakedness. The hunting knife was missing. So was the sheath. So was the belt.

I staggered around for a few minutes, found a gate, leaned on it and brought my heart up. It helped, even though I still felt lousy. Out in the darkness a fox barked. Under my feet I could hear scurryings and rustlings. I squinted across what seemed to be a flat and endless landscape but couldn't see a single light. The hounds could have dumped me somewhere in Outer Mongolia for all I knew.

I indulged myself a little. I felt very sorry for myself.

Then I saw the sweep of headlights coming towards me.

It was quite a relief to know I was *not* in Outer Mongolia. That, even at this ungodly hour, some other fool was out and about. I did a quick dust-off, ran fingers through my hair, then planted my feet wide in the middle of the lane and promised myself that the damn car was either going to stop or run me down.

It stopped. The headlights blinded me and I heard a door open and close. Then one of the headlights was masked by the big man – Dilton-Emmet – and, when he spoke, he did nothing to disguise his annoyance.

'What the flaming hell are *you* doing here?'

'As somebody once said . . . it's a small world.'

'How the devil are we supposed to . . .'

'*Shut it!*'

I had had enough. I, Harry Thompson, am a man of reason. I am prepared to be tolerant. I am even prepared to be long-suffering. But even *I* have my limits. I had been tooled around to all four points of the compass. Indirectly, I had been responsible for the death of a well-respected acquaintance. Twice, I had been belted across the skull by some lunatic with a liking for blunt instruments. I had had *enough*!

I snarled, 'One day, my big and boisterous friend, some smart-arsed, moronic bastard will do to *you* what you've done to *me*. And, when that happens, if you glance at the side-lines, you'll see me there cheering the opposition like . . .' I closed my mouth. In dramatic parlance I think it is called a double-take. My eyes widened and, in effect, I repeated his own question. 'What the bloody hell are *you* doing here?'

'Get into the car.' The rumble carried an overlay of disgust.

'I mean, why the hell should . . .'

'Get into the damn car, Thompson. And start hoping they aren't one jump ahead.'

I'd had enough. After that single furious explosion the fight was out of me.

Head lowered, I walked slowly towards the headlights. As I opened the car door I noticed the make.

It was a Merc.

FIRST
STAGE

Monday, October 16th

3.00 a.m.

I have known men (so called) who retired easily. Could be they were *born* for retirement, spent their working lives in what amounted to semi-retirement and saw retirement as the goal at the end of a miserable, not to say useless, existence.

Such men are mere digits in the world's population. They marry other digits and produce lesser digits. They live, but they are no more *alive* than figures on a balance sheet.

Not I!

Retirement was forced upon me and I accepted it without grace. I was not *ready* to retire. I could think of nothing *worse* than retirement. My birth certificate told the world that I was well past the three-score year mark. My body called the birth certificate a liar. I was fit. I was active. My eye was as keen as ever. My brain functioned on all cylinders and my reflexes were as immediate as they'd ever been.

Neither was I kidding myself.

Nature had given me the constitution of an ox and the body to go with it. I enjoyed my booze, I enjoyed my cheroots. The old libido wasn't as hyped up as in the past but the joy of battle was still there and, for the last few weeks, I'd had some nice moments fighting big fish off the Florida Keys. The plan was to stock up the launch a group of us had hired and try for even better stuff in deeper water; to take off from our base on one of the islands, call in at Andros Island, then push on to Crooked,

Acklins and the Caicos group and end up somewhere in the Turks Island group and, from there, try the open Atlantic for size.

It was a great idea, but it wasn't for me. The telephone bell in the beach bungalow we were renting changed *my* direction immediately.

'D-E?' I recognised the voice of my old boss, Peter Jones.

'Speaking.' I clawed at my beard, then ran fingers through my hair to bring on full wakefulness. On principle, I grumbled, 'This is one hell of a time of night to be making British Telecom rich.'

'It's a moderately civilised hour at this end.'

Peter Jones didn't give a monkey's. He never had and never would. He'd been (probably still *was*) boss-man of the tiny outfit I'd joined after Hitler's war. Just a handful of us, paid via the back door to do jobs neither MI5 nor MI6 fancied. There had been a certain amount of loose-knit discipline . . . but not much. Jones had received his orders verbatim (and not over a telephone wire) from some top Whitehall office. He'd worked out the general strategy and, in turn, had told whoever he fancied for the job what was required. Where necessary, he'd done the fixing and, thereafter, stepped from stage centre.

The chosen goon had done what had to be done, knowing that everybody (including Jones) was going to deny everything if the damn thing came unstuck. We all knew the rules and accepted them. Moderate luxury at the government's expense if things went smoothly. But if we lost balance we'd be left to stew in jail, or if necessary be guillotined, garrotted, decapitated, fried, hanged or shot. It was one way of learning how various civilised nations discouraged too much naughtiness.

It had been an unusual occupation and I'd enjoyed myself.

That's what I'd been forced to retire from, and now my

90

old boss had traced my whereabouts and was telephoning me at the most God-forsaken hour of the twenty-four.

'We need you back here,' he said.

'"We"?' It was a question he wasn't going to answer, but I couldn't resist asking it.

'Half-eleven, this evening. Gilliant's office.'

'How in hell's name can I . . .'

'You can . . . just. If you get the nits out of those whiskers. Your ticket will be waiting at the Pan Am desk at Miami.'

The phone went dead and, as I dropped it back onto its prongs, I grinned.

The bastard was right, of course. I *would* come running. I couldn't *not* come running. All the blood and muck that had made life interesting. At least, *my* life.

It sounded as if I was coming out of 'retirement'.

11.30 p.m.

I sipped the triple whisky Gilliant had had the sense to serve me and, for the moment, I listened.

Jones was there, of course. And, needless to say, Gilliant. Gilliant was now big bwana of a bloody great conglomerate of coppers, with his flash office in the northern city of Lessford. He had become very civilised. Not like the old days, when he'd been the link between what *we* were and official law-enforcement; when *he'd* done all the arresting, without asking awkward questions about ways and means, or what had happened before.

I liked Gilliant. Even as the somewhat staid, top-ranking copper, I still liked him. I had him measured. Underneath the braid he was still the same Gilliant. I could see it in the glint of his eyes. In the slightly forward tilt of his body as he listened to the others and soaked everything – legal

91

and illegal – into a mind that was a damn sight better than an ordinary policeman's mind.

Young Campbell was saying, 'It's more than a simple snatch-and-grab-the-money situation. If they demand what we *expect* them to demand we're in real trouble.'

'That,' said Jones, 'is what your father says. It's why we're here.'

'Yes ... but can we *do* anything?' The chap seemed worried.

'Mr Campbell.' Gilliant glanced first at Jones then at me. 'With these two characters around, something *always* gets "done" ... something, or somebody.'

'It's a kidnapping,' said Jones, firmly. 'That's *all* it is. *They* want to pump it up into an international incident. The Shamoan government deny all official knowledge.'

'Governments are paid to know damn-all.' I contributed.

'I believe them. It's the usual set-up. A government holding on by the skin of their teeth. A rebel faction champing at the bit to take over and line *their* pockets. And this bloody dam. If the rebels can make this dam project look like a school pantomime they can get some real mileage out of it. *That*, for Christ's sake, is Shamoan politics.'

'Where is Shamoa?' Gilliant asked the question. He looked almost embarrassed. He ought not to have felt embarrassed. It wasn't a country much in the news.

'North-west Africa.' Jones handled the geography lesson. 'Hemmed in by Algeria to the north, Mauritania to the west and Mali to the south. Nobody wants the infernal place. It hasn't a coastline. It's on the southern edge of the Sahara. Little vegetation ... not a hope in hell of an agricultural economy. Not much mineral deposits. It's just *there*, and it's short of everything we in the West take for granted. The dam would help stabilise the place. But that's what the rebels *don't* want.'

'They're crazy.' Campbell sounded very upset. 'They

92

kidnap my kid sister and expect *that* to help. What the deuce can *we* do to . . .'

I closed my ears to the conversation for a while. I had the gist of what the problem boiled down to. I'd travelled a long way and that, plus a certain amount of jet-lag, fogged the brain a little. I caught odd snatches of conversation, but left the others to do the conversational to-ing and fro-ing.

'From what your father says, they sound educated enough. That doesn't make them any less dangerous, but . . .'

'Surely to Christ the Shamoan government know who their opponents are. They could name names. Even if they leak a few off-the-cuff-details . . .'

'Alex, old son, Her Majesty's Government don't *want* to know. We've enough bloody hassle in that part of the world, without having to formally . . .'

'A cool million. Plus. The "plus" addendum is the worrying part. We can guess what that is, but . . .'

'Jones, I'm only a chief constable. Even to be *here*, and not report this conversation, puts me out on a limb. I'll do what I can, but . . .'

I think I must have dozed off for a few moments. Could be I was starting to snore – they tell me I do, sometimes – but I was brought to full consciousness by Peter Jones bawling me out.

'You're in this too, y'know, Dilton-Emmet. We haven't paid your fare all the way from America just to give you the benefit of drinking English beer.'

'All right.' I forced myself to take some interest in things. I was still bad-tempered when I continued, 'All right. Let's all stop stroking the damn cat. Let's grab a handful of fur and make it howl for a change.'

'I don't see . . .' began Campbell.

'A million cabbage leaves. Can your old man deliver?'

'I've already said. It's not . . .'

'Hell's teeth!' I snarled. 'Let's keep it simple. Don't jump the gun and worry about what else they *might* want. Can he deliver the million?'

'Yes. It's all ready. Fives, tens and twenties, in used and unmarked notes.'

'That,' I observed, 'must be a sight to see.'

'It takes up a lot of room. I don't know how . . .'

'It won't be a suitcase switch,' I growled. 'It won't be a carrier-bag change-over. It has to be delivered, or it has to be collected.'

'I don't see how that . . .' Young Campbell chipped in again, before I'd time to finish.

'There's a Joe Muggins,' I snapped. 'There's a go-between. From their side, or from our side. Somebody who collects and delivers the ransom. *We* decide. That gives us a slight edge.'

'What . . .' Young Campbell was very worried. He waved his arms a little. 'What if *they* decide, first?'

'We tell them to go screw themselves,' said Jones, bluntly.

'Look, we *can't*. We can't . . .'

'We *can*.' I upped the decibel rate. 'We bloody well *shall*. Sonny, that's the only lever we have. They don't want your damned sister. What good is she to *them*? They want the money. Then they want the cancellation of the contract.' I lowered the volume and continued, 'The Shamoans. They're from a continent – a certain *part* of that continent – and people from that part of the world *don't* shove women on pedestals. Harems. Concubines. All right . . . they don't make a big show of it these days, but it's still there. It's part of their history. Part of their culture. Women are second-class citizens. They *still* are. That's one argument they can understand. That we don't give too much of a toss about your sister and that, if we *are* going to play ball, *we* choose the go-between.'

'I – I don't like it,' moaned Campbell.

'With appropriate subtleties,' murmured Jones.

'With subtleties,' I agreed.

'I – I still don't like . . .'

'All right!' I exploded. 'Pay the bloody money. Don't build the blasted dam. They'll oblige. They'll tell you where to collect your sister . . . but the chances are she'll have her throat cut.'

Tuesday, October 17th

1.00 a.m.

I walked back into Gilliant's office.

I'd needed air. Even what passed for air in a place like Lessford. I'd left the other two to argue with Campbell. For my money he was a stupid young pup, without the basic gumption to know when the opposition had teeth they were prepared to use.

His old man, Sir Douglas Campbell, obviously knew people in high places; had met up with Peter Jones at some point in his life and, when Mary Campbell had been lifted, had had the sense to contact the one man able to help.

He hadn't passed his brains down to his son!

This, in the crazy parlance of the day, was a 'hostage situation'.The Bill Sikes type had no part in this set-up. It was top class and being organised by the brand of criminal prepared to handle hi-jacking, bomb-planting and the like. Terrorists, if you like – 'freedom fighters' if you care for double-talk – but, whatever, men to whom the odd corpse left bleeding in some dark alley was par for the course.

Young Cambell hadn't yet grabbed that much of the truth.

I had left Jones and Gilliant to draw the stupid young fool diagrams.

Less than twenty-four hours previously I'd been able to walk to the beach, tilt my head and see more stars than a man can count in his lifetime. Tonight it was hard to see the moon beyond the glare from the blue-tinged street lighting. This, too, was part of the price demanded for the only job I cared a damn about. To cross the double-crossers. To terrorise the crowd whose coinage was terror.

We could do it, Jones and I. We'd had practice. What we *couldn't* do was haul passengers along. Especially reluctant passengers.

I walked back into Gilliant's office and didn't mince words.

'Campbell. We do things *our* way, or not at all. These creeps have to be out-smarted. You! You couldn't out-smart a four-year-old at Happy Families.'

'I – I only want to help,' he bleated.

'Fine. Help by keeping quiet.'

'Hey, Dilton-Emmet . . .' began Gilliant.

'Nor do we want coppers in on this act.' I dropped down into the chair I'd vacated before my walk. 'Present company excepted, but every flatfoot I've ever met *looked* like a flatfoot, *talked* like a flatfoot and *acted* like a flatfoot.'

'Ultimatums?' Gilliant cocked a sardonic eyebrow.

'Just that,' I agreed. 'Or, if you like, professionals versus professionals.'

'Policemen are "professionals".'

'Gilliant, we're not talking about some kinky bastard who's nicked panties from a clothes line. We're talking about fanatics. We're talking about . . .'

'We're talking about law-breakers.' Gilliant was snapping back, but that was okay. I liked Gilliant. I admired him. Take that crappy uniform away and he was all man.

'The girl's life is in danger. To prevent her from being killed . . . Number One Priority. But not the *only* priority. I want the kidnappers standing in a dock. Who the hell they are – Shamoan, home-grown, who the *hell* they are – they taste British justice, that or it's all a waste of time.'

Jones jumped in before I could argue the man down. And, because Jones was still the boss, I listened.

'Back to the go-between . . . He was using that cold drawl I'd heard in the past. It was a voice that slapped him straight back into the driving seat. 'Not you, D-E. . . . you're too damn conspicuous, and somebody might recognise you from the past. Not you, Campbell . . . you're not reliable enough. Not you, Gilliant . . . you can't take indefinite leave from this office without some hot-shot Police Committee member asking questions.'

'You?' I suggested, sarcastically. 'Is that it? Are you putting your own name at the head of the list?'

'Don't be idiotic.' He glared, but it didn't impress me. As far as *I* was concerned we were well past the 'glaring' stage of this drawn-out chit-chat session. He continued, 'I'll be in the background, pulling strings . . . as always.'

'As always,' I agreed nastily.

'Don't let your tongue get *too* beefy, Dilton-Emmet,' he warned. 'You, of all people, should know the score. Upset me too much and I might be tempted to pull the *wrong* string.'

'I think . . .' Gilliant stepped in and lowered a fast-rising temperature. 'I think that's about as far as we can go tonight. Why don't you leave things with me? I'll find you the go-between.'

'Not a copper,' I growled.

'Somebody . . .' He paused to chuckle. What he was thinking seemed to amuse him. 'Somebody you can manipulate. It's what you two excel at . . . manipulating

97

people. Leave that side of things with me. I'll find you a sucker.'

The way he mouthed that last sentence made it a very offensive remark. I glanced at Jones, but Jones seemed satisfied and Campbell hadn't had a say in things for some time. I was too tired to kick-start another argument.

7.30 a.m.

'Blackpool.'

I glanced at the digital clock on the bedside table and wondered whether Gilliant had lost what few marbles he still possessed. To telephone a guest at one of Lessford's better hotels then open the conversation with the name of a candy-floss holiday town didn't make much sense.

'You know who's ringing?' he said.

'I know.' I reached for the cheroots and matches. 'I just don't know *why*.'

'Last night.'

'This *morning*,' I corrected him.

'The conversation touched mugs.'

'With "A Present from Blackpool" painted on the side?' I suggested. I was getting into the swing of things. I lighted the cheroot and waited.

'A present I think you'll appreciate.'

Double-talk – triple-talk – old Gilliant hadn't lost the knack. We were back at the old game. Never trusting a telephone unless it had a scrambler attached . . . and, even then, not trusting it *completely*.

'The Golden Mile?' It wasn't a question. It was a lead-in, meant to give Gilliant room enough to play conversational footsy.

'You'll find a better one on the North Pier.'

'Thanks.' I drew on the cheroot. I asked, 'How big?' . . . meaning 'When?'

'Four-and-a-half inches' ... meaning 'Four-thirty, today'.

That was all I needed to know. We were back with the old ball game and the years seemed to drop from my shoulders. To trust nobody. To be devious for the sake of sheer deviousness. Nor, at a guess, did Gilliant mind. For a few minutes we talked garbage to each other. We mentioned non-existent aunties and uncles. We exchanged false memories of family reunions which had never happened. It was padding. It was also practice; a polishing-up of a technique, in case it should be needed in the near future.

That telephonic exchange convinced me. Something rather special was simmering on the hob and, if it boiled over ...

I bathed, dressed and wandered downstairs for breakfast.

As I boned my second kipper the hall porter walked into the dining room, came to my table and said, 'Mr Dilton-Emmet?'

I smiled up at him and nodded.

'The man from the garage has just delivered your car, sir.' He dropped the keys onto the table-cloth. 'He tells me the fault's been found and rectified. It's waiting for you on the hotel forecourt.'

'Thanks.'

I picked up the keys. The leather-bound tag gave the number of the car. The make was a Mercedes-Benz. I knew the tank would be full. I knew a Certificate of Insurance and proof of ownership would be in the glove compartment.

I knew Jones. He never did things by halves.

4.30 p.m.

Some clown coined the phrase 'The Las Vegas of the North' and it sounded good. Good ... but all to hell.

I knew Vegas. I knew Blackpool. Any one of the big gambling joints in Vegas scooped more loot in a week than the whole of Blackpool pulled in a season. Blackpool 'closed down' in November until the weather improved. Vegas whooped it up twenty-four hours a day for ever. Vegas was crooked. Blackpool was merely naughty. Vegas was a whore practised in every trick of her trade. By comparison, Blackpool still wore petticoats and pantaloons.

Nevertheless . . .

That damn North Pier took all the clout coming off the Irish Sea and, size for size, the Irish Sea was as nasty a piece of salt water as any going.

I shoved my hands deeper into the pockets of the wind–cheater and hoped whoever was here to meet me believed in punctuality.

The drive across the Pennines had been pleasant enough. The Merc had lived up to its reputation as one of the class cars of the world. It had just about everything, including a built–in telephone and, as I'd expected, I could 'prove' it was all mine.

Meanwhile I stood there, in the gathering dusk, staring up the coast towards Norbreck and Bispham, wondering what sort of prat Gilliant had come up with. Some dumb-bell . . . obviously. Not a copper. I'd made that very obvious. I didn't want to be lumbered with a 'police mind' if things warmed up. I wanted somebody I could con but, at the same time, somebody who could be . . .

'They said a large man, with a red beard.' I turned as the words were spoken, and the man continued, 'I'd say that description fits you.'

'Walk along the prom,' I growled. 'You'll find half a dozen answering the same description.'

'All of whom know Chief Constable Gilliant.'

I stared down at the man. He wasn't a small man, yet

he gave the impression of smallness. He looked what I later discovered he *wasn't* . . . insignificant. On the other hand he looked quite calm. Quite unruffled. Very sure of himself in an unspectacular way.

'Gilliant?' I wasn't yet quite sure, and I had to *be* sure.

'I've been tailing you since you parked the Merc.' He smiled.

'The hell you have!'

'I've been following you since you hit the M55.' The smile widened.

I waited and, without fuss, he gave the registration number of the Merc, the name of the Lessford hotel where I'd picked it up and the exact location of its present parking spot.

'Let's assume,' I murmured.

'No.' He shook his head. 'Let's be *sure*.'

He took a wallet from his inside pocket and produced his identification. Detective Chief Inspector Lyle. The warrant card was no imitation and the photograph removed any last doubts.

'I said "No coppers",' I sighed, but fished out the driving licence and passport I'd taken from the glove compartment of the Merc, and handed them to him for examination.

'No coppers,' he agreed as he handed back my papers. 'Gilliant made that clear. He was asking around. Men he knew. Men he trusted. I came up with a suggestion, and he seemed to like it.'

We walked from the pier and turned right along the promenade. The illuminations were switched on and the town was picked out in hundreds of thousands of dancing, swinging, racing fairy lights. 'The Greatest Free Show On Earth' was how the publicity people billed it . . . and it was.

We talked of a man called Harry Thompson; a one-time investigative journalist; a creep who was smart

101

enough to dig deep, but not smart enough to dig deep into *himself*.

'He cracked up under the pressure.'

'Weak,' I grunted.

'No. Just *a* weakness. He believes in the hard-man-soft-centre theory.'

'They aren't around.'

'Not for long,' smiled Lyle.

From the end of the Central Pier – from the peak of the Tower – coloured laser fans shimmered and swung. Beyond the tram tracks the traffic was reduced to a crawl as vehicles eased themselves, nose-to-tail, through a tunnel of gaudiness. Kids and passengers pointed. The poor goon at the wheel kept one eye on the car in front and the other on the engine temperature.

'You think this Thompson character could be a go-between?' I asked.

'He could be conned into offering himself.'

'Conned?'

'He could be tricked into volunteering.'

'You interest me.' This Chief Inspector Lyle was no run-of-the-mill flatfoot. 'You've already given it some thought?'

'With Gilliant. With a mildly slippery character called Jones ... and with Campbell's son. While you were catching up on your sleep.'

Out there on the prom it was as private as Antarctica ... and damn near as cold. The old conjuror's trick of distracting attention was being pulled a hundred times a second. Crowds all around, but who noticed two men strolling along by the rails of the promenade with all the changing patterns of light in every direction. We talked in low voices, but only the two of us listened.

Some dump called Rogate-on-Sands; part of another police district and the home base of this Lyle boyo. He was wasted there. He was wasted in the Police Service.

I could see Jones's hand behind the set-up – maybe a touch of the old Gilliant magic – but the finer details had to have been polished up by the man on the ground. By Lyle.

'Pink ribbon,' I grinned.

'Complete with tinsel ... if necessary.' He returned the grin.

7.15 p.m.

I didn't make it back to Lessford.

Somewhere west of Gisburn the car phone buzzed and I recognised Jones's voice.

'Manchester Airport,' he said. 'I'll meet you there.'

'What the hell is ...'

'As soon as possible.'

I turned right at Gisburn, took in Nelson and Burnley, then hit the M66 for the biggest built-up area in the north.

Wednesday, October 18th

8.00 a.m.

'I, too, have a boss,' snapped Jones.

'Who? God?' I was in no mood for pleasantries.

'The Foreign Office people are twisting my tail.'

'The Foreign Office people,' I reminded him, 'are blissfully ignorant of what the hell goes on. That's the stance they're taking. They can't have the bun *and* the cherry.'

'You know better than that.'

'Much more of this, and ...'

'As much as they care to throw at us,' he rapped. 'It's

what we're here for. It's why *you* came out of retirement with such a rush.'

'All for the sake of a teenage schoolgirl.' The disgust was there because that's how I felt.

'All for the sake of a dam,' he corrected me. 'The infernal place was once part of the Empire. It's now part of the Commonwealth. Some of the Whitehall crowd think it has a certain strategic value.'

'It has,' I growled, 'about as much strategic value as a boil on the arse.'

'*We* don't reach those decisions.'

'Look at the bloody place.' I glanced out of the aircraft window at the ground we were flying over. 'Perfect for a re-make of *Lawrence of Arabia*. That, and sod-all else.'

'Keep those opinions from Hakim.'

'Hakim Al-Mokanna,' I mused, bad-temperedly. 'Very matey. Likes to be known as "Hakim, The Saviour of Shamoa".'

'There are worse people.'

'Of course . . . but not much, and not many.'

'For Christ's sake, Dilton-Emmet!'

'All right,' I soothed. 'I'll not start anything. We're in the Republic of Shamoa. We're flying through Shamoan air space. We don't want an international incident.'

'We want the girl back,' said Jones. 'Her Majesty's Government want that dam built.'

'In that order of priority?' I sneered.

'Just keep your mouth shut, Dilton-Emmet. Your mouth shut, and those hands of yours in your pockets.'

'Would you like me to lick his boots?'

8.20 a.m.

The Republic of Shamoa.

A steel-fisted dictatorship pretending *not* to be a steel-

104

fisted dictatorship. Main vegetation – on the few square miles capable of producing vegetation – esparto grass. A handful of badly tended olive groves. A few poverty-stricken attempts at tobacco growing. Toss in some cork trees, some evergreen oaks, some Aleppo pines, some cedars and some cypresses and, after that, rock, sand, filth and thirst. Roughly a little more than fifty thousand square miles of rock, sand, filth and thirst with a single river meandering its way from east to west. A few streams, but only one waterway worthy of the name 'river'.

One of those tin-pot 'resurgent' countries, once upon a time tribal territories but, since a long-forgotten hint of oil under its soil, a place up for grabs by any self-opinionated clown with a yen for small, but absolute, power.

Hakim Al-Mokanna was merely the latest in a whole string of European-educated megalomaniacs eager to feather his personal nest via loot from HM Government. The crappy place had been living on tick since the natives had learned to wear socks.

And now Hakim wanted to build a bloody dam!

'It will,' he said, 'give my people hope.'

We were in what had once been the administration block adjacent to a transit air-strip built by the RAF during Hitler's war. Beyond the window a row of ancient Nissen huts gave proof of the run-down state of the place.

'You see, Hakim . . .' Jones wiped sweat from his face with an already soaked handkerchief, 'Campbell's daughter has been kidnapped.'

'I am told.'

Hakim stood there, slim but greasy, with his pencil moustache making him look like a half-caste Ronald Colman. His Savile Row suit had creases only where it *should* have creases. The Arab head-dress could have been an ad for Persil whiteness.

'We are,' he said, 'in a somewhat volatile state.' His

teeth were as white as his head–dress. 'The dam would help stabilise the situation.'

'Campbell's daughter has been kidnapped,' repeated Jones.

'By terrorists from my country.'

'They would call themselves "freedom fighters",' murmured Jones.

'Mr Jones . . .' (He almost pronounced it 'meester'.) The teeth took another quick airing. 'First the dam. Then a hydro–electric plant. Thereafter, electricity. Five years from now, my country will be exporting manufactured goods to your country.'

'Real London School of Economics stuff,' I growled.

'Dilton-Emmet!' Jones rapped the warning, then returned his attention to the Shamoan. 'Hakim – take my word for it – Campbell won't even start the dam until his daughter's been returned to him . . . unharmed.'

'In that case . . .'

Hakim raised a finger. It was pure ham, but it was meant to impress.

The two goons wearing camouflage suits and berets doubled to within hearing distance. The Usi sub–machine-guns slung from their shoulders were not there for decorative purposes. I'd recognised their type from the moment they'd flanked Hakim on his arrival at the air–strip. Like the rest of his crap-arsed kind, Hakim Al-Mokanna had an élite corps personal bodyguard; men prepared to kill or die . . . not, necessarily, for *him*, but rather for the good life offered whilever they kept him upright and healthy. They did their job well – they always do – because, come a national change of heart, *they* would be the first to be slammed against a wall and shot. Somewhere there was a rear exit through which Hakim could bolt when the kitchen caught fire. But it wasn't available to these heroes. These bully-boys would be lucky if death came quickly.

Some sort of signal passed between Hakim and his

back-up duo. One of them doubled out of the room and, within a minute, returned hauling a quaking piece of humanity whose torn clothes, bruised flesh and terrified eyes were proof that, already, *he*'d been threaded through the meat-grinder.

'My enemy's friend,' smiled Hakim.

'Therefore, *your* enemy,' I murmured.

Hakim beamed at Jones, and said, 'Your large friend knows the sayings of my country.'

'An Arab saying.' Jones glanced at the trembling newcomer. 'Who is he?'

'A friend of *your* enemy, Mr Jones. My information is that he knows about Sir Douglas Campbell's daughter.'

Jones nodded, slowly, then turned to the captive.

'Is that true?' he asked, and I'd never before heard his voice carry that amount of compassion.

The captive's eyes darted from face to face, but he remained silent.

'You have my word,' said Jones, gently. 'Help us find the girl – tell us where she is – and you'll leave on the plane with us. You'll be safe.'

'I – I – I am not sure, sir.' The man had some difficulty in speaking. Split and swollen lips, combined with a dry mouth, made the words mumbled.

'Somewhere?' encouraged Jones.

'In your country . . . somewhere.'

'My country? England? Or the United Kingdom?'

'Your country. England . . . I think.'

'England. Whereabouts in England? Which *part* of England?'

'From – from place to place . . . I think.'

'Can you help us?' pleaded Jones.

'Please . . . that is all I know.'

'That is what he says, Mr Jones,' purred Hakim. 'That is *all* he says. We have interrogated him . . . at length.'

Jones stared directly into the prisoner's face, and said, 'There is safety. I can promise you safety. There will also be a reward – a very large reward . . . I can promise you that, too.'

'She is in your country,' moaned the prisoner. 'She is moved. All the time she is moved. That is all I know.'

Jones sighed and nodded. He turned to Hakim.

'That's it, then. Not *quite* a wasted journey, but not much to go on.'

'And this?' Hakim moved his head in the direction of the prisoner.

'He's your countryman. For what little additional information he's been able to give . . .' Jones shrugged his resignation.

'He will,' said Hakim, 'tell my enemies what he has told you.'

'That's a risk we must take. Keep him in prison until I've . . .'

Jones's voice was drowned by the burst of fire from one of the Usi SMGs. Even I – and God knows *I'm* used to both handling and hearing firearms – jerked with startled surprise at the suddenness and the magnification of the noise in the confines of the room.

The shots sent the prisoner a full three yards before he hit one of the walls, spun round and bounced on the concrete floor . . . by which time he was well and truly dead.

As the room cleared of sound Hakim said, 'He was the enemy of my friend. Now he will tell nobody.'

There was a silence, then I snarled, 'We must meet again, Hakim Al-Mokanna. Just the two of us. In the privacy of one of the dark alleys of the world. A final discussion on friends and enemies.'

Thursday, October 19th

Every man to his poison – every man to his opinion – but I have never subscribed to the theory that anger is a destructive emotion. A man who cannot rage is a man incapable of genuine outrage; he seeks to excuse the inexcusable; he mumbles half-hearted psychological clap-trap; his God – assuming he has a God – officiates at jumble sales, Mothers' Unions and cheese-and-coffee mornings. My God – assuming *I* have a God – demands that the scales of justice remain balanced and that I, and my kind, make damn sure they *do* remain balanced.

The unnecessary slaughter of a helpless prisoner had changed things. Hakim Al-Mokanna had shifted this kidnapping caper onto a more personal level.

This, then, was at the back of my mind as we lunched in a private room of the Beaconsfield on that Thursday. It would remain at the back of my mind until I had sent Hakim Al-Mokanna on a journey to make peace with *his* God.

Jones was there. Lyle, the local detective chief inspector, was there. Young Campbell was there. We tossed ideas into the kitty and I learned a little more about the abduction of old man Campbell's daughter.

'Why couldn't he warn Mary?' It was a crazy question, and a question with an obvious answer, but young Campbell wouldn't accept the answer. He repeated, 'Why *couldn't* he warn Mary?'

'For Christ's sake!' I growled. 'Your father did what he could. He grabbed you and your girl-friend from under by the skin of your teeth. Thirty minutes later and they'd have had two – maybe three – bargaining counters. Your sister wasn't get-at-able. Don't blame your father. He got the tip-off. He acted. He did what he could . . . don't ask for more.'

'If it could only have been me, instead of her . . .'

'Campbell!' Jones made it like a slap across the face. 'If you can't contribute, don't hinder. We're here for a purpose and that purpose is *not* to waste time telling each other things we already know.'

Jones was annoyed. Jones could go screw himself. Quietly, or with bands playing and flags waving. On the flight back from Shamoa – on the drive from the airport to Rogate-on-Sands – I had made that clear. I had explained to him in clear detail that he was no longer the boss-man he'd once been. Having forced me into retirement then, having hauled me back into the stewing pot, he was handling a different breed of animal. I took instructions, but I no longer blindly obeyed orders. Of late, I had found myself gathering certain principles – a luxury I'd been obliged to deny myself when 'officially' under his control – and I'd grown to take kindly to a life which included such principles. I would, eventually, return to that life, and the hell I was going to sling those principles into the ash-can merely to please Jones.

'He sent word he had a man who could give us information,' he'd snapped.

'What information?' I'd stormed. 'If ever there was a wasted journey . . .'

'We had to go. What option had we? Hell's teeth, man, we've so little to go on, we *had* to take a chance.'

'I will tell you.' I'd glared and growled as I'd made my little speech. I'd done nothing to hide my feeling. Nor had I seen any reason for hiding them. 'The murdering bastard merely wanted to *demonstrate*. To show what he could get away with. To warn us – Campbell, you, anybody – that to arse around with his precious dam would get the blood flowing. That lives don't mean a thing. The life of the poor sod he had murdered, or the life of Campbell's daughter. In Shamoa *he* is the only power worth consideration . . . and we'd better remember that. *That's* why he had us in his God-forsaken country.'

'The object,' Jones had snarled, 'is to plug what might develop into an international embarrassment.'

Then, I'd told him what *my* 'object' was, and the argument had flared and died continuously until we'd reached Rogate-on-Sands and been met by Lyle and young Campbell.

Lyle interrupted my memories by saying, 'Why not?'

We all stared our incomprehension as a slow smile reached up and crinkled the corners of Lyle's eyes.

'Why *not*?' he repeated. 'Why *not* let the world at large think you've been kidnapped? Why not use *you* to make Harry Thompson bite on the hook?'

'Not "the world at large",' warned Jones. 'Whatever you have in mind, we want it to be as close to the chest as possible. We have the girl to think of.'

Lyle nodded his understanding, then popped the first good idea into the pot. We played around with it for a while – pro-ing and con-ing, adding and taking away – until we ended up with a moderately workable scenario.

Eventually, I said, 'Even with the kinks ironed out we'll be knitting gossamer. You . . .' I turned to young Campbell. 'You'll be handling the star role. You'd better be good . . .'

'If it helps Mary, I'm prepared to . . .'

'. . . You'd better do more than *play* at not knowing what the hell's happened to you. To do the job right, we'll have to knock you around a little.'

'Is that necessary?' Lyle turned 'copper' for a moment.

'It's all right,' Campbell urged. 'I don't mind.'

'Yes, Chief Inspector. It's necessary. I'll get onto Sir Douglas, this evening. Get his backing.'

That's how, where and when the brainwave was conceived. We didn't know it, but we'd accidentally timed it very sweetly. We'd given ourselves maybe another week before the kidnappers made any sort of move. They weren't

111

crooks in the accepted sense of the word. They figured themselves patriots ... and maybe they were. Coppers, like Gilliant and Lyle, take a different view of things. To them, a crime is a crime is a crime. A simplistic belief which goofs up the real truth. It means you label some great men as criminals and some prize prats as saints.

Me? *I* decide who are the ungodly. I need no rule book. I need no Parliamentary debate.

I had already reached a decision about the crowd who'd snatched the Campbell girl.

The goods they'd taken would be returned either undamaged or dead, and the choice was left to old man Campbell. They needed the money, to fund opposition to friend Hakim, but the cancellation of the dam project was their real aim.

That was *my* decision, but it was a very lonely decision. The others didn't share it. The others figured the snatch crowd as little more than tin-pot crooks out to feather a personal nest.

I almost hoped to hell they were right.

Friday, October 20th

9.00 a.m.

This Harry Thompson character had been chosen as the patsy, therefore it seemed right and proper that I stay within reaching distance. Reaching distance meant Lytham St Annes and one of the Best Western Hotels International group of hostelries. The Clifton Arms had a pace which suited the tail-end of jet-lag plus a quick nip to North Africa and back. I caught up with the clock in very civilised surroundings. The Merc was parked out front and a quick drive down the coast would bring me to Rogate-on-Sands in no time at all.

The window of the dining room looked out on the estuary of the Ribble and a gloomy day, with rain which looked as if it was here for a prolonged stay. Gulls huddled together in groups on the green which separated the road and the prom, and passing cars trailed a cloud of fine spray in their wake.

'More coffee, sir?' The waiter stood with coffee and hot milk at the ready.

A refusal was already forming on my lips when I saw Jones's car pull onto the apron in front of the hotel.

'More coffee,' I agreed, then added, 'And an extra cup, please. I think I have a guest joining me.'

Somebody in the foyer directed Jones to the dining room and as he folded himself onto a chair at the table, he said, 'They've been in touch.'

'And?'

'Sir Douglas wants you to take over all communication.'

'The hell with that.' I sipped from the refilled cup. 'We agreed upon this Thompson guy. We've already . . .'

'Not the go-between.' Jones spooned brown sugar into his coffee. 'The mouthpiece. The man keeping tabs on the delivery and the collection.'

'It will,' I grumbled, 'be more like a blasted procession than a switch.'

'You can do it.' The grin was meant to make us buddy-buddies again. It didn't but, knowing Jones, it showed how much influence this Campbell creep had. Jones added, 'You can do just about *anything*.'

'Now tell me the good news,' I sneered.

'London.' He tasted the coffee. 'Charing Cross Hotel. Three o'clock in the Betjeman Room..

'Who am I meeting? Miss Joan Hunter Dunn?'

'He'll find you.'

113

'I am,' I complained, 'doing one hell of a lot of hithering and thithering .'

'You've a good car at your disposal.'

'I want Thompson well and truly hooked.'

'Hooked and gaffed,' promised Jones. 'I'll handle that side of things until you get back.'

'*When* I get back,' I murmured.

'Tonight. Your bed, here, will be waiting for you.'

'*If* I get back.'

3.00 p.m.

The Merc had been a dream to drive. Every horse under the bonnet was a thoroughbred raring to go. I'd taken the motorway route and the journey had lasted less than three smooth-riding hours. Lunch at the hotel, a stroll around the corridors and through the bars, a quick, but thorough, check outside and in the gloom of the adjacent railway terminus. All very basic stuff. If you're working solo on a tricky assignment it is as well to know who, or what, is behind you. Nobody has the job of guarding *your* back.

There'd been nothing . . . nothing obvious. On the other hand, had it *been* obvious they wouldn't have been the professionals I figured them to be.

I couldn't win!

Therefore, I sipped tea and waited.

The Betjeman Room. A nice, airy room, overlooking the Strand. Beyond the room-length picture-window flags of various nations angled out and fluttered over the passing pedestrians. Scarlet double-deckers swallowed and spewed passengers. London cabs scurried in and around the rest of the traffic, like a swarm of angry black beetles.

I enjoyed a cheroot, tasted tea and looked down on a city which seemed to be bursting at the seams.

Behind me and just within earshot two WI types

voiced plummy inconsequentialities about a wedding;
passed photographs; tried to out-do each other in
marriage-ceremony minutiae.

They lived in their own little world.

Come to that, so did I . . . and my world was far more
crazy than theirs.

'Good afternoon, Mr Dilton-Emmet.'

He slipped into a spare chair at the table, placed his cup
of tea on the surface and smiled across at me. He was very
civilised. And why not? He was obviously a very civilised
man. Shamoan, certainly. But I liked his cut. He was both
polite and sure of himself, but he wasn't arrogant.

I nodded a greeting.

He said, 'You, I understand, represent Sir Douglas
Campbell.'

'That's what *I* understand.'

'A certain proposition has been put to Sir Douglas.
You know about it, of course.'

'I know about it,' I agreed.

I liked the man, but I had a job to do. *He* was going
to set the pace.

He was wise enough to realise this, and he said, 'There
is a project Sir Douglas has in mind. Presumably you know
of *that* project, also.'

'Of course.'

'And?'

'He still has it in mind.' I drew on the cheroot and gave him what I hoped was an enigmatic
smile.

'There is also a certain cash transaction.'

I nodded.

'Is he, at least, happy about *that*?'

I lifted the cup to my lips, raised a sarcastic eyebrow,
and murmured, 'Happy?' I tasted the tea, then added, 'In
his shoes, would *you* be happy?'

'I chose the wrong word.' The apologetic smile was

calm enough and friendly enough. 'Is he – shall we say
. . . *agreeable*?'

'He thinks the price is a little high, but he's prepared
to pay it.'

'Good.' We were talking about lives. We might have
been discussing double-glazing. 'And the project we were
talking about?'

'Ah . . . the project,' I murmured.

I put what I hoped was a worried look on my face and
listened to the WI biddies trying to out-brag each other
in the wedding-breakfast stakes.

My companion said, 'We must talk about the project, Mr
Dilton-Emmet.'

'At the moment,' I said, 'the project must continue.'

'That is a great pity.'

'I think Sir Douglas might agree with you,' I lied.

'In that case . . .?'

'These things,' I hedged, 'tend to generate their own
momentum. Once they're under way, they are as difficult
to stop as they were to start.

'Nevertheless . . .' He waited politely.

I waffled happily along and said, 'It should be done. It
will be done . . . if it's at all possible. Meanwhile – and as
evidence of good faith – the price will be paid.'

There was much of the same stuff. Neither of us mentioned the subject-matter of our meeting, but neither of
us needed to. To say that we argued – even gentlemanly
arguments – would be an exaggeration. He was quietly
asking for everything, but was wise enough to know he
wouldn't *get* everything. I, on the other hand, was fishing
around trying to tease some sort of information out of
him.

I ordered fresh tea and, as I spooned sugar, said, 'The
goods you have on offer tend to bruise very easily.'

'Not with careful packing.' He smiled.

'Sir Douglas wouldn't be interested in damaged goods.'

'My dear Mr Dilton-Emmet.' It was a slow and sad accompanying smile. 'We have given much thought to the matter.'

'And yet, you wish to sell sight unseen.'

'I suppose . . .' He moved a shoulder before tasting the fresh tea. 'I suppose arrangements could be made. It might be difficult.'

'But, not impossible?'

'Is *anything* impossible?'

I could have named a few things but, instead, I said, 'A mutually acceptable adjudicator?'

'Mutually acceptable?' There was doubt and, perhaps, suspicion in the question.

'There must be somebody,' I urged gently.

'If *I* name a person *you* will be suspicious. If *you* name a person *I* will be suspicious.'

I nodded my understanding.

'In that case . . .?'

'We have,' I said, carefully, 'given some thought to this.'

'Naturally.'

'Somebody we can both trust.'

'Is there such a person?'

'Thompson. Harry Thompson,' I murmured.

'I know of no such man.'

'Nor do I.' I squashed what was left of the cheroot into an ashtray. 'I only know the name.'

'An employee of the Burns Civil Engineering Group?'

'That,' I said, 'would be particularly stupid.'

'Why not you . . . personally?' he asked.

'Because that's what *I* am.'

'What?'

'An employee of Sir Douglas Campbell . . . albeit on a temporary basis.'

It seemed to satisfy him. It wouldn't have satisfied *me*, but maybe Lady Luck brushed my shoulder at that moment.

After a few moments of hesitation, he said, 'Tell me about this Harry Thompson.'

I told him as much as I knew and he listened very carefully. What I didn't tell him, of course, was that Thompson was also a hand-picked sucker. The old left-hand-not-knowing-what-the-right-hand-is-doing technique was something I'd learned under Jones's tuition and, although I liked this fellow well enough, he represented a crowd I was being paid to out-smart. On a personal level, I didn't give much of a damn about the final outcome of these back-door shenanigans, but Campbell's daughter was in there somewhere, and I was being paid to look after *her* interests.

'One thing,' I warned. 'This Rogate-on-Sands dump. It's not like here in London. You'll be asking around. Checking on Thompson . . .'

'Of course.'

'My guess says the skin pigmentation might make you more than a little conspicuous. Especially at this time of the year.'

'We have English friends.' He smiled.

'It might be wise to use them.'

His lips bowed into a quick smile of acknowledgement. The point had had to be made, despite the touchiness of the subject matter.

And that was just about all. He left and I stayed in the Betjeman Room until around four, in order to give him time to get clear, and to let whoever was there check time to satisfy himself that I wasn't playing follow-my-leader games.

Then I hoisted myself from the chair, stretched my cramped limbs and strolled back to the Merc.

The WI types were discussing possible names for the first baby as I passed their table.

Saturday, October 21st

8.30 a.m.

In civilised surroundings, I am a man who likes to start my day in a civilised manner. I like my breakfast to be a slow and tasteful meal. I like to linger a little over the toast and marmalade; to taste that last cup of coffee and inhale deeply on the first cheroot of the day. Dammit, yesterday Jones had rushed me through the tail-end of the meal and now, today, Lyle was yammering on about the bait having been taken. He was not too excited. Merely infernally self-satisfied.

'Lyle.' I interrupted his stream of *amour propre*. 'It's happened. It was *meant* to happen. If it hadn't happened the whole blasted exercise would have been a waste of time. Meanwhile, my breakfast is spoiling.'

'I thought you'd like to know.' He sounded slightly miffed.

'So? Now I know. Now we *both* know ... plus any clown who might be hooked in on this line.'

'Oh!'

'Why not make *absolutely* sure? Why not put a small ad in the local newsrag? Set it to music and have the LSO include it in their next concert.'

I slammed the receiver back onto its rest and returned to my interrupted meal. The trouble with coppers – especially *honest* coppers ... they can't be trusted. Mix them up with some mild jiggery-pokery business and, if it comes off, they're like kids with a toffee-apple farm. Already the opposition could have somebody snooping around Rogate-on-Sands. Asking questions. Keeping tabs. Detective Chief Inspector Lyle might already have binoculars trained on him.

Jesus! Amateurs in this game *always* cause problems.

119

I finished my breakfast in peace and, on my way to the lift, the receptionist called me over to the desk.

'The telephone, sir.' She motioned a well-manicured hand towards the handset whose receiver was already off its rest.

I grabbed it and started, 'Look, Lyle, if you can't . . .'

'Go for a drive towards Blackpool.' Jones's voice cut in on me. 'Make sure you're alone.'

'Sure.'

The phone was dead before my one-word answer had reached the mouthpiece.

Jones, of course, was a *professional*.

Noon

The De Havilland touched down at twelve o'clock, precisely, and Jones hurried across the grass to greet the occupants.

Me? I'd been a mite surprised to learn that Blackpool *had* an airport. The call had come through on the Merc's telephone.

'Meet me at Blackpool airport at fifteen minutes to twelve.'

Jones's voice, and I'd been driving a few miles inland from the coast; twisting and doubling along the country lanes; belting around double bends, then pulling in at some field entrance in order to let any following car drop a clanger by catching up on the blind spot. Nobody was on the trail and I'd pointed the Merc's bonnet towards Lancashire and the Fylde district, towards an airport I'd never heard of.

Squires Gate, on the southern end of Blackpool. Appropriately sandwiched between a holiday camp and a damn great fun-fair. It was, it seemed, one of those penny-ante air-strips used by people bopping around between the

Fylde coast, Ireland, Manchester, Liverpool and the British Gas platform anchored off shore.

For its size it was a busy little dump and 'security' would have had Fred Karno nodding immediate approval.

I'd left the Merc in the park, strolled into the pint-sized lounge and joined Jones at one of the windows.

'I could,' I remarked, 'have driven a lorry-load of explosives into this place. Who's it run by? The IRA?'

Jones grunted a non-committal reply. It wasn't *his* stamping ground, so why should *he* care. He followed the approaching executive DH with his eyes, then spoke.

'He's here.'

'Who?'

'Sir Douglas Campbell. Who else?'

'Who else?' I sighed, but Jones was already leaving the lounge to walk across the damp grass and towards where the plane would end its taxiing run.

I stayed where I was. I was reaching the conclusion that I was being told as little as possible, and I was damned if I was going to do a puppy-dog act. What they wanted me to know they'd tell me. What they *didn't* tell me wasn't likely to deprive me of too much sleep.

Jones returned with two strangers. I guessed the tall, worried looking one was some sort of yes-man. *He* was carrying the brief-case, whereas the thick-set character with the opened overcoat and the mop of iron-grey hair had those pale, forget-me-not blue eyes favoured by killers and hot-shot businessmen.

'Sir Douglas Campbell. Dilton-Emmet.'

Campbell nodded. He didn't acknowledge the introduction and he kept his hands behind his back. That was okay by me. I didn't even nod and kept *my* hands in the pockets of the wind-cheater.

'There's a place,' said Jones. 'Down by the prom. A car park. It's rarely used at this time of year.'

Campbell snapped, 'Lead on. We'll walk.'

121

We walked. It wasn't a long walk, but the tall guy evidently had some trouble breathing. Maybe asthma . . . something like that. Nobody gave a toss about the tall guy, and if he wanted to kill himself in the service of his master, who was I to say him nay?

It was a very exposed car park. A sort of hidden-away full stop at the end of the prom and the tram-lines. How in hell Jones *knew* about it puzzled me a little but, for sure, it was an ideal spot. Beyond the wall the Irish Sea tried to knock the stuffing out of the base of the prom.

The wind nipped inland and carried an occasional flurry of spray. And that was it – the wind, the spray and us . . . we were in a miserable little world of our own.

'This man Thompson.' Campbell wasn't the man to waste time on pleasantries. 'Can he be trusted?'

'He's gullible enough,' said Jones. 'At least, that's what Lyle thinks.'

'Lyle?'

'The local chief inspector.'

'I made it perfectly plain,' barked Campbell. 'No police in this thing. Damnation, Jones . . .'

'Gilliant recommended him,' cut in Jones. 'And I, for one, trust Gilliant's judgement.'

'He's a good man,' I added . . . it being time *I* said something.

'How the deuce can you make any sort of assessment, if you've only just . . .'

'We're not putting him up to be Queen of the May.' I figured it time Campbell realised he hadn't cornered the market in bad tempers. 'We're making him Sucker of the Month. We don't *need* to trust him. He doesn't know what the hell's happening to him . . . at least, not yet.'

'You think you can handle him, then?'

'Campbell . . .' I lowered my voice in order to emphasise my irritation. 'An educated guess suggests that you already know my record. Jones will have told you,

122

before dragging me into this thing. A man like you ...
you'll have double-checked. I don't *think* I can handle this
Thompson character. I *know* I can handle him. Him, and
a dozen like him. At a pinch, *you* and a dozen like *you*.'

'Very sure of himself ... isn't he?' Campbell looked at
Jones as he asked the question.

'It's just that ...' Jones began.

'I like him.' Campbell tightened his lips, switched his
glare in my direction and nodded. It was meant to make
me happy. It made me even more convinced that the man
was a jumped-up popinjay. 'You'll do as my representative.'

'Meaning?' I grunted.

'Use him – this man you say you've hooked – use him to
get my daughter free. Offer him a retaining fee of a thousand a day.' He made a snapping motion with his fingers
and the tall man fished a cheque from the brief-case and
handed it to Campbell. 'Five thousand. Offer him that,
for openers.'

I took the cheque and tucked it safely away while I
waited for His Nibs to do some more pawn-moving.

He said, 'Nobody gets me at either office or home
without specifically asking for Extension Four-One-Two-
Three. Telephone the registered office, day or night, ask
for that extension ... you'll contact me, wherever I am.'

'Neat,' I admitted.

'We'd better have some sort of identification phrase.
Just in case the wrong person *does* sniff things out.'

'I refuse to make a fool of myself,' I grunted.

'Good God, man. All I'm ...'

'That,' I growled, 'is as good an identification as any.
"I refuse to make a fool of myself." It's a bloody sight
better – and more natural – than waffling on about ducks
flying backwards at midnight, or tooling around whistling
the opening bars to "Danny Boy".'

'I like him.' Campbell smiled for the first time. He
smiled at Jones, and repeated, 'I *like* him.'

123

Jones looked slightly less enthusiastic, but kept his mouth shut.

Thereafter we talked in the usual circles for another fifteen minutes or so. Campbell threw his weight about a little, but that was to be expected; he was footing the bill and it was *his* daughter who'd been kidnapped. As with his son, the infernal dam loomed far too large in his conversation, but that was to be expected . . . dams and the like were where his millions came from.

Nobody made a specific suggestion that we should return to the airport. By mutual, but silent, consent we all seemed to agree that we'd said everything of any real importance and, at that point, we seemed to gently ooze our way from the car park, across the prom and over the bridge towards the airport entrance. Nobody had checked us leaving. Nobody checked us going back in.

5.00 p.m.

The ex-Mrs Thompson underlined one very obvious fact. Harry Thompson – a man I was already manipulating, but a man I had yet to meet – didn't know when his bread was buttered. The 'ex' bit proved that. She was some sort of legal type, but without a hint of mustiness. Dark, trim, neatly turned out and with more than her fair share of common sense.

'Why Harry?' she asked.

'Why *not* Harry?' I countered. 'One thousand smackers for each day's work doesn't make him cheap.'

'He isn't *that* talented.'

'Could be you're selling him short,' I suggested.

'You . . .' She smiled. '*You* might be worth a thousand a day. You're the type. But not Harry.'

'Harry Thompson,' I mused. 'Private detective. One-time investigative journalist.'

124

'*Failed* investigative journalist,' she corrected. 'The pace was too hot. He cracked.'

'This time, he won't crack,' I promised. 'This time, *I'll* hold his hand.'

'Therefore . . . Why me?'

To me it was obvious. To her it wasn't too obvious. And it was a little difficult to explain.

We shared the front seats of the Merc. It, and her own car, were parked on a lay-by about five miles inland from the coast. It was a B-class road and Lyle had fixed the meeting at my request, and after he'd told me about the ex-Mrs Thompson. Dusk was moving in and, across the water-logged fields the lights of a farmhouse were switched on.

'Somebody Harry Thompson can trust,' I said gently. 'Somebody *I* can trust. A communication link . . . one that *he* doesn't know about.'

'And if I tell him? About this meeting? That he's being "used"?'

'You won't.' I was sure enough to sound certain. 'You think too much about him.'

'Too much about him to allow people like you to . . .'

'Too much about him to deny him the chance to regain his self-respect,' I interrupted.

'He's no coward.' She jumped in there on the defence.

'Lady . . .' I waved a hand. 'There's a phone. This jalopy has all mod cons. Pick up the phone. Dial your ex-hubby. Spill the beans. Everything.' I paused, then added, '*That* . . . or do him a favour and help *me* to look after him.'

It took her about thirty long seconds to reach the decision I already knew she'd reach. She was a nice kid. She was rather proud of this creep she'd once been married to. More than that, she was still crazy about him. She was anxious for him to pick up the pieces which the breakdown had knocked off.

Thereafter, I told her the tale. Strictly speaking, not the

125

whole truth, but as near to the truth as made no matter.

I pulled the con that there'd been a double-kidnapping and that young Campbell had broken loose.

'He's lost his memory,' I lied. 'Harry visited him in the local hospital this morning.'

I had to tell her as much as Thompson might tell her, but *not* tell her what I didn't want *him* to know. It was tricky. It was a little like throwing away a yoyo and still keeping a tight hold on the string.

'He doesn't know who young Campbell is, just yet,' I said.

'But you do?'

'Lyle does . . . but Lyle has orders from up top to keep his mouth shut.'

'In God's name, why?'

'Medical reasons,' I said, vaguely. Then, 'Instructions from old man Campbell. If the kidnappers start hunting around, trying to retrieve him, we might be able to grab them.'

'It sounds very dangerous,' she muttered.

'Not with your help. My job is to ride guard on Harry, without the kidnappers – without Harry – *knowing* I'm riding guard. That's where you come in. Harry's a nice guy, but not yet too sure of himself. He'll try to guard his back. He's not yet ready to go completely solo. He'll let somebody into the secret. Somebody he can trust. You.'

'And *I* tell *you*?' There might have been contempt in the question.

'Unless, of course, you don't give a damn *what* happens to him.'

That was the ace of trumps, and I played it in a very off-handed style. It won me the game, without too much trouble. Love – *their* brand of love – is said to be blind. It is also deaf, dumb and stupid. She hummed and hawed a little, but she'd already swallowed the bait with the hook attached.

126

'I contact Lyle?' she sighed, at last.

'You contact Lyle,' I agreed. 'Every day, and always from a telephone kiosk. You use the name "Liz" and you use the name "Harry". No surnames. Just where "Harry" is, what he's doing, what he's said and what he plans. That will keep *me* alongside him.'

Sunday, October 22nd

I had the gismo fitted to the Merc. Standard surveillance equipment, James Bond for the use of. Miniature directional aerial in the roof-space, receiver unit and screen on the dashboard. Plus magnetised transmitter unit to clamp cunningly onto the metal surface of the car to be followed.

Jones did the necessary arranging and poured scorn on this basic back-up gimmick.

'Oh, my word!' The telephone wire did nothing to hide the sneering tone. 'What next? Code books and secret ink?'

'I'm prepared to use false noses and paper hats if it might help,' I growled. 'Once this Thompson character hits the tall timber I need as keen an edge on things as possible.'

I was the man at the sharp end and, despite his lordly disdain, Jones was pro enough to realise that. *I* called the shots . . . otherwise, *he* carried the can.

He was professional enough to know that, too.

That Sunday, the Merc was collected from the hotel forecourt and was back in place before dusk. In the glove compartment were three matchbox-sized transmitter units ready and eager to grab and hold any metal surface they came in contact with.

Monday, October 23rd

I drove out to Rogate-on-Sands. I parked the Merc, pocketed one of the transmitters and asked around for a dining/drinking place called the Wine Bibber. That (according to Lyle) was where this Thompson boyo lived; next door to and above this boozer-cum-café.

I located it. I even paused long enough to read the brass plate which told the world that this was the stamping ground of the Thompson Detective Bureau. A 'bureau', for God's sake! We were handling some nut with an FBI complex.

Lyle had told me that Thompson parked his car somewhere at the rear of the Wine Bibber, but it wasn't there.

I began to worry.

Anybody capable of calling a one-man snooping outfit a 'bureau' is just about capable of anything. He could have been contacted. He could have gone beefing out into the wide blue yonder on a one-man rescue campaign. He could be stiffening in some hedge bottom. Anything!

I found a kiosk and told my troubles to Lyle.

We strolled an almost deserted prom and he quietened my immediate fears.

'He's not a fool,' he assured me.

'I only have your word for that.'

'He's neither a fool nor a glory-seeker.' He turned up the collar of his mac against the weather. 'He damn near tumbled to young Campbell's "loss of memory" gag.'

'Holy cow! All the young idiot had to do was look dumb and claim not to know . . .'

'He combed his hair,' sighed Lyle. 'Thompson loaned him the comb. He smoked a cigarette. Thompson offered the packet. I don't know too much about these things, but *does* a genuine amnesiac know how he wears his own hair? And the fact that Campbell didn't bring his heart

128

up clued Thompson in on the fact that Campbell isn't a non-smoker.'

'*Not* a fool,' I agreed gently. Reluctantly.

'And other things.' Lyle smiled. 'You've met his wife?'

'His ex-wife.'

'That young lady wouldn't have married a fool. And, if she had, she wouldn't still be in love with him.'

'Is she?'

'We're both banking on it.' He glanced at his watch, then suggested, 'We'll have a meal. My treat. Then we'll have a drive out to the "Pull and Nor".'

'What the hell's the "Pull and Nor"?'

'The Pullbury and Norton Rifle and Pistol Club. Thompson's a member. Tomorrow should see him there for his monthly session.'

'A Dead-eyed Dick?' I murmured.

'I'm told he's not a bad shot.'

'I'm impressed,' I growled. 'This Thompson boy of ours has hidden depths.'

Lyle, too, had hidden depths. He'd hunted around at the local libraries and found a copy of a recent *International Construction* with a group photograph which included young Campbell receiving an award on behalf of Burns Civil Engineering Group.

'Thompson almost had him.' Lyle's chuckle showed he was enjoying this cat-and-mouse game more than, as a copper, he should. 'It was there, in the way he talked. He *almost* had him.' Lyle opened the magazine at the required page and ran a thumb down the division. 'Leave it on a table at the "Pull and Nor". Our lad seems to make a day of it each month – a general social-club atmosphere – the chances are he'll spot an oddball publication in a lounge where only newspapers and shooting journals make up the reading matter. He's nosey. Comes from investigative journalism, I suppose. He picks it up and, with luck, it opens at the right page. Bingo! He knows who the mysterious stranger is.'

'And?' I wasn't following the devious meanderings of the mind of this most unusual policeman.

Lyle said, 'Fingers crossed. If *he* comes to *us* . . .'

'We've nailed him,' I pointed out. 'He doesn't have to "come to us". He's already been nominated.'

'Ah! But if he doesn't *realise* that . . .'

I didn't argue. It wasn't worth it. This Machiavellian obviously had a mind like a monkey-puzzle. He was like a kid with a new toy; he had to work it until the batteries ran out or the wheels dropped off.

I waited in the car while he delivered the magazine to the club. I smoked a cheroot and pondered upon the worries of a man like Sir Douglas Campbell; a poor little rich man able to hand out a cool million, without even feeling the pinch, for the return of his darling daughter. I decided that, when the account was submitted for my services, I must make quite sure he knew he was paying for the best.

We returned to Rogate-on-Sands. Thompson's car was where it *should* have been. Lyle kept look-out while I clamped one of the transmitting gewgaws inside the metalwork of the rear bumper.

Before we left, Lyle said, 'A few days ago – when we first met – I suggested that friend Thompson might be tricked into volunteering for this thing you have going. He's half way towards volunteering. He'll go the full distance, once he *knows* something. At the moment, he only suspects . . . and isn't even sure what it *is* he suspects.'

'I'm a simple man,' I grunted.

'I don't make that claim.'

'With good reason.'

'Simple, or not, you're big,' he warned. 'Conspicuous. You stand out like a tart in a monastery. You, and that flash car of yours . . .'

'You're too kind.'

'. . . therefore, I suggest you leave the initial stages of this exercise to those who might blend into the landscape a little better.'

'You?'

'I'll let you know,' he promised. 'Thompson's already shown the sharpness of his wits. If he spots *you* treading on his coat-tails, all this softly-softly palaver goes right up the spout. You might as well have sent him a gilt-edge invitation.'

Tuesday, October 24th

5.30 p.m.

I sweated through that Tuesday. Lyle had been so right, but I didn't yet know Lyle well enough to trust him in this type of situation. As far as *I* was concerned, Lyle was still a top-drawer CID man; that, and nothing more. He tooled around with thieves, tearaways and perverts. His knowledge of international jiggery-pokery stopped short at the Bond films. For all I knew, *his* idea of surveillance was to plant a uniformed cop at the door of the Thompson Detective Bureau. That or become too laid back and miss the berk altogether.

Nor was Lytham St Annes the world's best place in which to forget immediate worries. Especially out of season. The wind was pumping itself up and the French Foreign Legion would have felt at home in the sand storm whipping across the road from the dunes.

I was seriously contemplating an after-dinner booze crawl when the phone in my room rang. I was, of course, in the bath. There is some sort of natural law which insists that people telephone other people when those at the receiving end are either sitting on the bog or naked and dripping.

Jones's voice said, 'Go for a drive at about seven.'

'Look . . .' But the line was dead and the only proof that the call had ever been made was the area of dampness on the hotel carpet. I muttered, 'Sod it!' and replaced the receiver.

It meant that dinner at the Clifton Arms had to be rescheduled but it was a class hotel and, no doubt, I wasn't the first awkward guest they'd had to cope with.

I finished my bath, dressed slowly, called in at the bar for a quick snort, re-timed my eating arrangements, then wandered out to the Merc.

7.15 p.m.

It had seemed a good idea to *go* somewhere. Footling around in an expensive car, going nowhere, has very limited appeal. I'd tasted Blackpool, I wasn't welcome at Rogate-on-Sands, I was already *at* Lytham . . . So why not Southport?

I wasn't too taken with Southport. Lord Street seemed to be busy busting a gut to be what it wasn't and ended up by being high-priced without being particularly high-class. Turn any of the corners and the gimmick-shops were there; tucked away, like soiled linen some expensive whore didn't want you to see. It was past sunset when I arrived and the fairy lights linked the poles along the prom; they swayed a little and looked very twee, but they lacked the damn-your-eyes brashness of Blackpool because that would have caused apoplexy among the colonels and their ladies.

It was that sort of place, with that sort of atmosphere.

I figured I'd seen Southport and didn't want to see it again as I nosed the car to a parking stretch overlooking what passed as sands. I smoked a cheroot and waited.

Jones's voice came over the car's telephone.

'The mug has bought it.' We were still talking round corners.

'When?' I asked.

'Earlier today. He recognised the young one and tried to contact the old one.'

'Recognised?'

'Nothing "official" yet.'

'And?'

'He's all yours.'

'Lyle?' I asked.

'You, me and the old one.' I could sense the annoyance in his tone because I'd mentioned a name. He added, 'A tight rein. I hope you haven't lost your touch.'

'Understood.' I acknowledged my slip, then asked, 'Does the mug know what he is?'

'He will do, when you tell him.'

Wednesday, October 25th

3.45 p.m.

Harry Thompson. He stopped being merely a name and, instead, became a hunk of flesh, blood and muscle. Not too much flesh and very little muscle but, when I burst in on him, he was human enough to bare his teeth a little.

He cooled down enough for me to ask, 'Why not tell Lyle who the amnesiac is?'

He claimed not to have any real reason for playing the cards close to his chest, but that was all crap. There was a reason, and the reason was his old job. Investigative journalists are like stage magicians: they wave their right hand around while their left hand does all the work. They go in for deception in a big way ... sometimes self-deception.

We played conversational footsie for a while, then I waved Campbell's cheque in front of his eyes and greed took over. It seemed wise to prolong the double-header-snatch con and, equally, wise to play games about keeping Lyle in the dark.

It was like taking candy from a sleeping child. Harry Thompson, Esq., was ripe for the plucking. All I had to do was shake the tree a little.

Thursday, October 26th

2.15 a.m.

Fifteen minutes earlier Liz had awakened me from sleep by telephoning me at the Clifton Arms. She'd been in something of a panic and I'd had my hands full convincing her to hold onto her girdle pending my telephoning *her* from a call-box.

I'd found a kiosk by the Post Office, rung, given her the number of the kiosk and asked her to dial *me* in order that we shouldn't be tooling around shoving coins in slots.

And now this ...

'You promised you'd look after him,' she accused.

What could I do but agree?

'You said he'd be in no danger.'

'Not quite that.' I tried to be reasonable, but who can reason with a worried woman at that hour? I said, 'A grand a day has to buy *something*.'

'He was knocked unconscious, for heaven's sake!'
'That's the "something",' I grunted.
'I don't like it.'
'You can't stop it.'
'I don't want him mixed up in this thing.'
'I thought you were only his ex-wife.'
'I don't see what . . .'
'What *are* you, exactly? His mother-substitute? And does he *need* a mother-substitute?'
'You're – you're evil.' She was almost sobbing.
'I've been called worse things.'
'You don't care *what* happens to him.'
'Lady!' I snapped. '*I* wasn't the one who smacked him across the skull.'
'I – I . . .'
'You say he's going to carry a gun?'
'That's what . . .' The sigh shuddered a little but, when she continued, her voice was more composed. 'Mr Dilton-Emmet,' she said, 'I'm worried sick.'
'He won't carry a gun,' I promised. 'We're having no OK Corral antics.'
'He has one at the rifle club. A pistol. I'm sure he'll try to . . .'
'He won't carry a gun,' I repeated. 'Now, don't lose any more beauty sleep. Take something – a stiff whisky, a tranquilliser, anything – and tuck yourself up for the rest of the night. You were wise to ring. I'll take care of things from here on.'

3.30 a.m.

Lyle was not amused. I didn't blame him too much. I'd buzzed Jones after I'd taken over the wheel of the Merc, and *he* hadn't done cartwheels of delight. Big deal! I was the mug at the sharp end, but I needed back-up, and the back-up included both Jones and Lyle. Jones had telephoned Lyle and Lyle had been waiting for me to pick him up outside the Beaconsfield.

Now, he was sitting alongside me in the Merc, smoking a cigarette and sulking.

'Unless,' I remarked, 'you fancy some clown prowling around your manor holding a loaded firearm in his fist.'

'The word "manor",' he grunted, 'is peculiar to the Met. Up here, we call it a "patch".'

'We live and learn.'

There was a Two Minutes' Silence in memory of the sleep he'd lost, then he said, 'Why *me*? Why the hell have *I* to hold your hand? Aren't you big enough to go out in the dark alone?'

'Both ways. Coming and going.' For a man who held rank, he was remarkably dumb. Could be he was still struggling to get both feet out of the Land of Nod. I expounded, 'Officially and unofficially. This steward of the gun club . . .'

'Cooke. Alfred Cooke.'

'If he scares easily . . .'

'If *you* sneeze at him, he'll be over the horizon before you've time to blow your nose.'

'Exactly.' I nodded my understanding. 'I want him scared . . . but not *that* scared. I want him on elastic . . . not in chains.'

'Did anybody mention that you're a devious bastard?'

'I know. It's part of my irresistible charm.' I stared at the road ahead and decided that the Merc really was a beaut of a car to drive. Even at this hour. With loot like this at your fingertips darkness moved from stage-centre into the wings. The road ahead was as well-lit as it would be at midday. I said, 'I want Thompson by the goolies, but I don't want him to feel me grab. Let him make his play. Let him congratulate himself upon being a smart little private eye. Then, when he's up to the neck in sewage, throw the brick at his head and see if he ducks.'

'You also have a neat turn of phrase.'

'The trick,' I explained, 'is to keep this Cooke character on edge. You're the red-necked cop. I'm the unknown quantity. He's scared of us both, therefore there's nowhere for him to run. We nail *both* feet to the floorboards. He knows we're using him, but he daren't *not* be used. What he *doesn't* know is *how* we're using him. Not even a hint that it's Thompson we have our eyes on,'

'Why?' Lyle blew out his cheeks. At a guess, he wasn't a man to sulk for long. He was a copper, therefore he was curious. 'Why the hell should Liz Thompson telephone *you*? Why not me? Okay – she did the right thing in letting somebody know her ex was getting gun-happy – but why *you*?'

'Obvious.' I grinned. 'The engine under my car's bonnet has more horse-power than yours.'

Alfred Richard Cooke. 'Alfie' to his friends, although anybody claiming friendship from this creep was in dire need of a companion.

I'd kept my thumb on the bell-push until a light had appeared in the living quarters above the club-house. A frightened voice had called from beyond the panels, Lyle had identified himself, the door had been opened and we'd strolled inside.

Alfie was certainly worth travelling a few miles to see. Turkish Delight slippers, complete with bobbles. Shanks no self-respecting dog would have wasted time burying. A shortie dressing-gown; artificial silk; a dragon motif against a background of peacocks, butterflies and impossible foliage. And from this Amazonian forest of impossible exotica poked a skinny neck, a bleary-eyed face and a thatch of uncombed hair.

'What – what – I mean . . .'

'Sit down, Alfie.' Lyle waved a hand towards an empty chair. Then, 'Sorry. Have we disturbed something?'

'I – I . . .'

'Interrupted something?'

'I . . .' Alfie swallowed, then muttered, 'I have a friend staying the night.'

'A friend?' Lyle's tone was edged with contempt.

'It's not illegal any more.'

'That depends.'

'It's not illegal. People can . . .'

'It depends on the *age* of the "friend".'

'He's – he's thirty . . . thereabouts.'

Lyle nodded his provisional satisfaction, then said, 'Don't sweat, Alfie. As you remark . . . it's legal these days.'

The poor bastard was as helpless as a fish hooked on the line of an expert angler. Lyle played him without mercy, then dumped him, exhausted and gasping at my feet.

'This is Mr Dilton-Emmet, Alfie. He is a terrible man. I promise you . . . a *terrible* man. You'd be well advised to listen to him very carefully. Listen, but don't question. And do *exactly* what he tells you to do.'

Lyle ended his introduction with a quick, warning nod then strolled out of the room towards where the stairs led to the living quarters.

'Members of this bang-bang organisation,' I growled. 'You'll have a list somewhere.'

'A – a card-index system, sir.' The sweat gleamed on his face and a trickle ran down the hollow where his neck joined his chest. 'It's in the office.'

'Show me.'

In the office, I solemnly performed the required pantomime. I fingered my way through the cards and made believe I wasn't yet quite sure about something. I chose four cards. Thompson's was one of them.

138

'These four members.' I waved the cards under Alfie's nose. 'I'm interested.'

'I – I . . .'

'You, little man, are going to help me satisfy my interest.'

'I – I don't know . . .' The creep was actually trembling. 'I don't know anything about them, sir. They're club members, but . . .'

'Just listen, Alfie. Don't *argue*.' Lyle had re-joined us. He glanced at the ceiling, and added, 'Lover-boy, upstairs. He's to be told *nothing*.'

'Oh, no, sir. I – I wouldn't . . .'

'You *would*,' contradicted Lyle, 'but you'd better *not*. If you *do*, the next time I see you will be for identification purposes on a morgue slab.'

'Jesus, Joseph and Mary!'

'This man I've introduced to you, Alfie – this Dilton-Emmet – he can do just that. He can blow you off the face of the earth. Snuff you out, like a penny candle. *And I can't stop him.* That's who he is, and what he is . . . and you'd be wise to accept what I say as no less than the truth.'

It was quite a high-powered sales pitch and, as he was making it, Lyle pulled a telephone directory towards himself and started to thumb through the pages.

Alfie's eyes popped and Alfie's mouth gaped . . . but Alfie was far too terrified to utter a word.

'These four members.' I took over from Lyle. 'Until I blow the whistle for time, I want to know everything they do whenever they visit the Pullbury and Norton Rifle and Pistol Club. Everything! Which guns they use. How many rounds they fire. How long they stay. Who they're with. If they so much as fart off-key, I want to know . . . and as soon as possible.'

'Yes, sir. Of course, sir. I'll – I'll . . .'

'As soon as possible, but without arousing their suspicion.'

'Yes, sir. I'll . . .'

'It shouldn't be too difficult.'

'Easy, or difficult, you'll do it,' contributed Lyle. He'd scribbled a number on the top sheet of a notepad. 'That's the number you ring. Day or night. Ask for our friend, Dilton-Emmet. And, for your own sake, I hope you do everything *exactly* as it should be done.'

5.00 a.m.

There was a distinct nip of frost in the air as we drove away from the gun club. It was still dark. Very dark; something about the darkest hour being just before dawn. Maybe, but the headlights countered that proposition. Come to that, the Merc's heating system shrugged off the touch of below-zero temperature. But I drove with the window slightly open and the slip-stream had tiny steel teeth. Outside, it was easing its way into long-john weather.

'Quite the hard-nosed cop,' I observed. 'I hardly recognised myself.'

'You recognised yourself,' grunted Lyle.

He sat hunched in the front passenger seat and stared ahead through the windscreen. His eyes had that glazed, faraway look of a man whose mind is on other things.

'I don't like it,' he growled.

I didn't know what the hell it was he didn't like, so I neither agreed nor disagreed.

About half-a-mile later, he muttered, 'The timing's too perfect.'

'The timing?' It seemed only polite to show some degree of interest.

'Sod's Law,' he continued and his eyebrows stitched themselves into a scowl. 'There has to be some degree of a balls-up, somewhere.'

'You're worried because we haven't come unstuck?'

140

'It happens.'

'It happens,' I agreed. 'I just don't get the idea of you *wanting* it to happen.'

'A thing *should* happen. I like it *to* happen,' he grumbled. 'If it *doesn't* happen, I get suspicious.'

He was a copper – an unusual copper, but still a copper – and his mind obviously ran along police tram-lines. It was the way they were trained to think. Nothing was what it seemed. 'Up' was merely a qualification of 'Down'. 'White' was a pale shade of 'Black'. Coppers! Every last one of them was crazy.

As we moved into the outskirts of Rogate-on-Sands, I asked, 'The telephone number?'

'Eh?'

'The one you gave Alfie, before we left?'

'Oh . . . that.' He seemed to make an effort and pulled himself out of his lethargical mood. 'The Beaconsfield.'

'What the hell good is that? I'm not stopping at . . .'

'You are,' he interrupted.

'What?'

'Lytham's too far away. I mentioned it to Jones when he telephoned me.'

'Look, I'm booked in at . . .'

'Not any more. Jones was going to cancel your room at the Clifton Arms. There's a bed waiting for you at the Beaconsfield. There's also a private garage booked.'

I wasn't pleased. This damned detective chief inspector had suddenly taken upon himself the role of puppet-master, and I was the dolly at the end of his string.

I snarled, 'Who the hell . . .'

'Cool it!' This one was no Alfie and very few times in the past had anybody rapped this brand of talk in my direction. 'You're a big man, Dilton-Emmet. You eat trees and spit sawdust. But what's going on happens to be very illegal and it's going on on my patch. Therefore, *I* set the pace. Okay, you're Jones's blunt instrument,

141

but I claim the right to know when you move into action.'

'Lyle! I don't take orders from . . .'

'From Jones,' he snapped. He touched the car's telephone. 'Give him a buzz. We had time to sort things out while you were on your way from Lytham. It proves my point. Thompson can be away and gone to hell before you're clear of the Fylde. I'm not the happiest man in the Northern Union. There's a stench, and I can't quite place it . . . yet. It might have something to do with Alfie. It might have something to do with Thompson. It might even have something to do with *you*. The limit has been reached as far as this particular police area is concerned. From here on, I keep a personal eye on things and, if anybody starts playing fancy footsie, I blow the whistle.'

8.00 p.m.

Coppers! Old women, forever testing the water at bath night. Never sure whether it's too cold or too hot. Everlastingly cautious and perpetually timid.

I had been determined to find fault with the Beaconsfield. On principle. If only because I was being buggered around without anybody having the good manners to give me a say in the matter. I was going to find fault. I was going to be a bloody nuisance. I was going to make my presence *felt*.

In the event, there was no fault to find and that in turn, stoked my frustration. The bed was big enough and comfortable enough. The food was classy, without being fancy.

Lyle had said, 'Thompson's front door is under twenty-four-hour surveillance.'

'That,' I'd sneered, 'should bring the Opposition out at full throttle.'

'From a distance. From behind closed curtains. Via binoculars.'

'So? Every damned copper in Creation knows all about . . .'

'In the force,' he'd interrupted, 'men obey instructions. They don't waste time asking questions.'

'Like bloody zombies.' I had been in a bad mood and had seen no reason to hide the fact.

Lyle had allowed himself a quick, tight smile. That was all.

A few hours of sleep had done good, as had a tasty meal of steak, kidney and mushroom pie, complete with trimmings. The coffee-and-cheroot stage had been interrupted by a call to the phone.

'The sucker has left his living-quarters.' I'd recognised Lyle's voice. 'He's not going far. He's carrying nothing. He hasn't even a mac with him.'

'Let's hope it doesn't rain.' I'd grinned, wickedly, then added, 'On second thoughts, let's hope it pisses down.'

Later – maybe two hours later – I'd been stretched out on the bed when Alfie had called. Thompson had taken his gun away from the club. It needed some sort of adjustment. But that was okay . . . he'd signed a 'disclaimer note'.

I'd had about an hour of peace before Lyle had contacted me again.

'The sucker's back home.'

'Is that a fact?' I'd made myself sound almost bored.

'He brought nothing back with him.'

'You have a strange idea of "nothing", Lyle.'

'Eh?'

'I'd call a loaded Walther P.38 quite *something*.'

'Jesus Christ!'

'Drop your anchor, Chief Inspector.' I'd rather enjoyed myself. I was repaying some of the hot-shot re-organising he'd done earlier. 'I'll see he doesn't do any damage with it.'

'I don't even want him to *have* it.'

'Fine,' I'd agreed. 'Leave things with old man D-E.'

And now I had the gun.

I'd walked around a little, found the Wine Bibber and, for a little while, contemplated a frontal assault. A straightforward going inside and taking the damn gun from him. I'd lighted a cheroot and weighed the scales a little. It would have given Thompson some slight edge, in that he'd have guessed that strict tabs were being kept on his comings and goings. That didn't *matter* too much. He'd learn the truth of things soon enough. But it seemed wise to keep the blinkers on as long as possible.

He'd solved the problem for me.

He'd left the dump he called 'home' for the downstairs wine bar. A judicious use of an Access card and, within minutes, I'd had the Walther tucked safely away in my pocket.

And now I was waiting. He'd returned to base and I wanted to check his next move.

The shadows were plentiful enough. Rogate-on-Sands, like most other seaside holiday spots, boosted the main-thoroughfare lighting but kept the back streets hungry for illumination. I could watch and, as long as I kept the glow from the cheroot shaded, know he wouldn't spot me.

He left the nest, but didn't turn off the light. He nipped back into the Wine Bibber, then back out and along the streets until he reached a telephone kiosk.

So, why a kiosk? I knew he had his own phone. The Wine Bibber had to have a spare handset, assuming *his* was on the blink. Something was scaring him . . . obviously. He was suspicious of wire-tapping . . . obviously. He was talking to somebody he didn't want people to *know* he was talking to . . . obviously.

I couldn't hear what he was saying, but I watched him feed coins into the meter. At the rate he pushed them into the slot, it had to be long-distance.

He returned home. His light was switched off. I ambled back to my own bed at the Beaconsfield.

I had that gut feeling – that slight tightening of the muscles around the solar plexus – something all men in my line of business know and take notice of.

Things were moving towards the start-blocks.

Friday, October 27th

4.00 a.m.

Alfie called. Alfie was in a muck-sweat. Thompson had just telephoned and Thompson had given the impression that he fancied Alfie's balls fried for breakfast.

'What do I *do*?' he wailed.

'*We* do,' I corrected him. 'Keep your legs tightly crossed until I get there. With luck I'll be there before *he* is.'

'But – y'know . . . what should I *do*?'

'Amuse yourself. Get a gun. A handgun. The biggest you can get your hands on. Load it, and have it ready.'

'Sweet Jesus! I'm not going to *shoot* him.'

'Just wave it around,' I advised. 'If I'm there first, *I*'ll wave it around.'

I dropped the receiver, climbed into some clothes and hurried down to the Merc. I was at the gun-club first. I had the car for it, I had the deserted roads for it and speed was something I was very used to. I'd parked the Merc on the blind side of the building, taken over the handling of a Colt .45 revolver and was ready for Thompson when he arrived. There was a certain amount of spit and vinegar thrown in Alfie's direction before I nipped Thompson's fuse and sent Alfie for an early morning hike.

Poor old Thompson. He was way above his own personal snow line. He huffed a little, puffed a little and performed a very amateur grumbling act, but the grand-a-day retainer fee was about the limit of his vision. It wasn't difficult. I sent him home convinced I had him where the monkey stuffs its nuts. He wasn't happy, but what the hell? He wasn't being *paid* to be happy.

9.00 a.m.

The thought struck me that, given a modicum of luck, one day I might actually eat my way through a breakfast without being called to the telephone.

But not this morning.

Thompson had left home with what looked like hand-baggage. Coppers and squad cars had been alerted; not to stop him, but to give some hint of his passage through the police area. He was believed to be heading west for the motorway network.

This was 'it' then – or so it seemed – and the Merc and its electronic gadgetry would, hopefully, do the rest.

The magnetised transmitter I'd clamped on the body-work of Thompson's car had a range of two-to-three miles. No more than that, and not even *that* when built-up areas and bridges created 'blind spots'. It was top-class equipment, but it was for real; it wasn't the dream-child of some flash movie script-writer with an excess of imagination. I had to get to *within* that range, otherwise I was merely burning petrol.

The time had come to make educated guesses. I plumped

for Preston . . . if only because the M6 skirted the west of that fair city. No doubt some of the traffic on that road out of Rogate-on-Sands will remember the passing of the Merc on that day: It was very necessary to push things, if only to reach transmitting distance before Thompson reached the tall buildings of the town, therefore I drove on brakes and accelerator and overtook with only inches to spare.

The blip appeared on the dashboard screen some few miles before we reached the outskirts. It came on too fast (again, these things don't happen in movies) and I was within two cars of Thompson's vehicle before I could revert back to more sedate driving.

That was okay. I had him hooked. I was in business.

There was a certain amount of merry-go-round crap in Preston itself. Maybe he'd spotted me. Maybe he was being ultra-careful. For whatever reason, he jumped the lights, doubled back on himself a few times and generally played hard-to-get.

Me? I followed up my first educated guess, made for the lead-in to the M6, parked and waited.

I had him. I let the blip pass, then followed him onto the south-bound carriageway and settled back to hide myself in the motorway traffic about a mile to his rear.

Noon

South of Junction 15 his speed eased. The blip on the screen became more pronounced. He seemed to be staying in the slow lane and allowing the HGVs to leap-frog him. It was a tricky situation, but that was okay . . . I was there to handle tricky situations.

147

I kept the Merc at a steady speed, kept my eyes open for the vehicles ahead and, eventually, spotted Thompson's car up front. I could *see* it. The ruse was to make sure *he* didn't see *me*.

I eased down on the mph, tucked the Merc behind a socking great ten-wheeler and did a certain amount of lane-nudging to give a periodic check that he wasn't suddenly taking off.

He moved into the slip-road leading to a service area and Lady Luck still rode alongside me. The driver of the ten-wheeler also decided to pull in at the same area.

From there, it was little more difficult than taking toffee from a kid. It was one hell of a car park and Thompson was a stranger. He tooled around looking for the entrance, then concentrated on parking his vehicle up by the building complex. I wasn't as choosy. I found a quiet spot, parked, then watched my quarry do what he was obviously expected to do.

He locked his car and made for the self-service restaurant. He was very nonchalant. A damn sight *too* nonchalant. The blue VW was the one car he *didn't* glance at. But his eyes flicked to the number plates and, as he passed, his fingers touched the bodywork.

I tell you! Men stalk tigers in the Indian jungles; they earn local fame because they know how the most dangerous big cat of them all behaves. But the tiger behaves instinctively. Man, on the other hand, *thinks*. He leaves no pug marks. There is no trail of carnage. But, if you can *see* the man you're stalking – if you can *watch* – and if you have the experience and have done it often enough, the 'pug marks' are there. The boffins call it 'body language' and they make believe they've only recently invented it. Not so! Men like myself have practised it for years. The way a man walks, the length of his stride, that hint of hesitation; what he does with his hands, the way he swings his arms, what he touches and what he doesn't touch; the way he holds his head, the things he looks at, the things he *should* look at, but deliberately ignores. With practice it is possible – even easy – to read the thoughts of a quarry and to be ninety-nine per cent sure of his next move.

Thompson's next move had something to do with the blue VW.

My next move was to reach the VW without Thompson seeing me.

From the Merc I could see him in the restaurant. I watched him eat a sandwich, drink tea and smoke a cigarette. From where he sat he could see the VW. He could *not* see his own car.

I pocketed one of the magnetised transmitters and allowed Mother Nature to make things easy for me. Thompson had driven a long way – the best part of two hundred miles and, to my certain knowledge, he hadn't left his car since Preston. Unless he possessed a reinforced bladder, he'd have a pee before leaving the service area.

As he straightened from the restaurant table I slipped from the Merc and made my way towards the VW. I bent for a moment to 're-tie my shoe lace' and the transmitter was in place. I nipped into the restaurant Thompson had left and, from the window he himself had used, watched him walk to the VW and drive away.

9.30 p.m.

The sucker was bedded down for the night at the King's Head, Aylesbury, and I, too, needed some shut-eye. I steered the Merc out of the town limits then buzzed Jones and shared my problem.

Jones, it seemed, could pull strings. We were within an hour's driving time from London and one of his minions took over watchdog duty on the VW while I booked in at the Shoulder of Mutton at Wendover, about five miles away.

Saturday, October 28th

1.45 p.m.

It was nice to be told. Come to that, it had been nice to have had a full night's sleep in a comfortable bed, followed by a genuine – and uninterrupted – English breakfast. That had been nice – *very* nice – and I'd returned to Aylesbury a much-refreshed man.

Thereafter it had been the same old Chase-Me–Charlie routine north along the A5. Thompson had stopped for a snack, but that hadn't presented problems. I'd raced past the café, noticed his parked VW, then belted ahead for the first turn-off past the café to give him a few more heads start.

That was when Jones had buzzed me.

Everybody skipped the double-talk. Maybe Jones had some flash, modern scrambler at his end, but at my end I was pretty sure it was plain speech. Jones obviously didn't give a damn. Neither did I.

'He's making for the service area north of Junction 38 on the M1. Get there before he does.'

'I'm already ahead of him, waiting for him to catch up.'

'Get there first, D-E.'

'No sweat. What's the problem.'

'The problem is Jerry Bankhurste.'

'Jerry Bankhurste!'

'Thompson's wife rang Lyle. Lyle notified me. He's meeting Bankhurste at the service area at half-four.'

'For Christ's sake! Does he *know* Bankhurste? Has he any idea what sort of a louse Bankhurste *is*?'

'Investigative journalism.' Jones's voice was sneeringly bitter, even over the air-waves. 'Crusading knights on white chargers. Thompson's met him a couple of times. The usual thing . . . a Fleet Street by-line almost amounts to deification.' I heard the expulsion of breath as Jones blew a silent whistle of disgust. 'Get there first, D.-E. Don't let Bankhurste screw things up to hell.'

4.00 p.m.

Jeremiah Bankhurste, 'Esq.' I will tell you about the 'Jerry Bankhurstes' of this world. They are the pariahs of the Fourth Estate. Because of what they are and because they represent the Press, they are told things. Sometimes little things. Sometimes big things. But always *confidential* things; things they should *not* be told. The good reporter – the good columnist – has a conscience; he recognises and rejects the sour-grapes tip-off; he weighs the good against the bad, the snide against the sincere, and writes only that which he believes should be made public. But not so the 'Jerry Bankhurste' types. To them, everything is of value. Everything! They dig, they worm, they grub around in all the muck they can find . . . then they give an option.

'Pay up, or I publish.'

Not money, you understand. Nothing as crude as straightforward cash. These bastards – the handful around – handle power. They trade the suppression of information for more information. They spin webs of leaked confidentiality; they enmesh scores of good men in a network of trivial indiscretions.

They figure themselves as king-makers, and the truth is that some of them end up with a Minister of the Crown in their grubby little hip pockets.

151

Bankhurste was one of their number and I was waiting for him when his Aston Martin zoomed into the service-area parking lot. I ducked out of the Merc and met him as he walked towards the restaurant.

'Bankhurste,' I growled.

He stopped, stared, then said, 'Do I know you?'

'You do now,' I assured him.

'What advantage is that to *me*?'

'Given half a chance,' I murmured.

'What?'

'You'll turn it to your advantage.'

'I'm damned if I know . . .'

'*I* know *you*,' I interrupted. 'I know *of* you. I know all *about* you. Obviously, Thompson doesn't.'

'Thompson?' I don't think he meant his eyes to narrow, but they did . . . very slightly.

'You have a shocking memory for names?' I mocked. 'The man you're here to meet. His name is Harry Thompson.'

'Just who *are* you?' he demanded.

'I'm not Harry Thompson,' I grinned.

'One of Campbell's heavies,' he accused.

I chuckled and let him live with his mistake.

'I can't be bought.' He meant it to sound arrogant, but the hint of a splutter tended to spoil the effect. 'I can't be frightened.'

'You can be frightened,' I promised him. 'You already *are* frightened . . . just a little.'

'If you think . . .'

'I think,' I said, 'we'll take a quiet stroll.' He hadn't been expecting it, therefore the one-handed wrist hold had not been difficult to make. I tightened my grip a little and he raised himself on his toes as the breath hissed past his teeth. 'A short stroll,' I continued. 'Without noise and without fuss. Any objections on your part, and you'll need major surgery before you can use that hand again. And, if anybody's watching, take my word for it, it will look as if you've fallen awkwardly . . . *very* awkwardly.'

'You can't . . .'

'As if you've fallen awkwardly, on the wrist,' I murmured. 'And, believe me, Bankhurste, I *can*.'

He believed me and he *could* be frightened. He *was* frightened. Not that he was a tough nut. These people never are. Their forte is the infliction of mental agony. They are in no way *physical*. I, on the other hand, am *very* physical . . . when necessary.

In the shelter of the HGVs in the lorry park I increased the pressure. With my free hand I slammed him against one of the cab doors, clawed my fingers around his throat and tilted his head up.

'Instructions,' I growled and, at every few words, I banged the back of his head against the metal of the door. 'Instructions from *me*, Bankhurste. You will blow. You will *not* keep your appointment with Thompson. You will forget Thompson and whatever snippets of gossip Thompson has already passed onto you. You will take the fastest powder you have ever taken in your miserable life. You have not even *been* here.'

I gave it time to sink in, then continued, 'These things you will do. Without question and without mentioning your visit here to a soul. You may then live a comparatively peaceful, but miserable, life. *Disobey* these instructions . . . and God help you! There's a vacant hospital bed waiting for you, Bankhurste. There's an operating table, with the surgeon already gowned and gloved. Go too far, and there's a hearse already being tanked up with petrol.' A second pause, then, 'Who *I* am doesn't matter. Merely that I am not your common-or-garden tearaway. You know – you, of all people, know – that men like me exist. And now you've met one. You've met one, and you've *lived*. Aren't *you* the lucky little bastard?'

As a final punctuation mark I slammed his head

153

once more against the side of the cab. This time I made it hard enough to knock him cold. I allowed him to slip to the ground in an untidy heap, then strolled back to the Merc.

5.15 p.m.

Thompson had arrived on the dot. He'd parked the VW and tooled around generally and it seemed that somebody was playing cat-and-mouse games with him. I'd noticed a couple of dark-skinned brethren busy doing nothing on the edge of the lorry park and, because Bankhurste hadn't yet shown his face and just *might* have more guts than I'd given him credit for, I'd decided to play Peeping Tom at closer quarters.

It was a good time of day. The heavy goods boys were taking their early-evening break and dodging between the parked multi-wheelers made keeping out of sight kiss-easy.

I'd watched the coloured boys while *they* were watching the VW. I'd seen Thompson stroll up to the car, to be met by one of them; noted the folded newspaper and known, from past experience, that it was a damn sight more lethal than a folded newspaper.

And now I knew the van and the registration number of the van, and the van had a magnetised transmitter firmly clamped to the underside of its metalwork.

I was in business again, and the words of the poor sod who'd been shot to ribbons on an isolated Shamoan air-strip made perfect sense.

'From place to place.'

In a bloody great furniture removal van. That was where the Campbell girl was. She was on wheels and she was for ever on the move . . . and now Thompson was in there with her.

I stayed in the shadows, watched the furniture van

move off then saw the sprawling figure by the giant artic. It was Bankhurste, and Bankhurste had ended his investigative journalism for one life. I didn't puke. I'd seen far too many stiffs to puke. But I made my way back to the Merc before anybody else stumbled over the corpse.

6.00 p.m.

We were, I decided, playing 'silly buggers'. I'd driven north from the service area, had thought the electronic bug had gone on the blink, then seen the furniture van on my right trundling towards my rear on the south-bound carriageway. And there are no U-turns on a motorway.

Junction 39 had been coming up fast, and that *had* to be where the furniture van had turned back on itself. I had done likewise and hared after the damn thing among the south-bound traffic.

I'd buzzed Jones and put him in the picture.

'Oh – and I think you should know – *I* didn't chop friend Bankhurste.'

'Has he *been* chopped?'

'Oh, yes. The fuzz should already be doing hand-stands at the service area.'

'That's one minor kink ironed out.'

'I'd already scared him off.'

'Whilever they breathe, there's always that hint of doubt.'

'You,' I'd remarked, 'are an unusually cold-blooded sod.'

'Of course.' He'd done nothing to hide the quiet chuckle. 'I thought we established that, years ago.'

Such a simple truth!

I am not given to spiders crawling up and down my spine but, while I steered the Merc south after the furniture van, thoughts and memories played tag with themselves. Jones. Hell only knew whether that was his real name. I, personally, would have bet money *against*, and I figured I knew him as well as any man alive. For more years than I cared to contemplate I had been Jones's 'big stick' – at a guess, only one of many – and when he wielded me I had always been safe. Jones had contacts, up to and including Number Ten – he was the ultimate Mister Fixit and if he couldn't fix it he removed it. He knew his way around the world better than most men know their way around their own back garden. Somewhere, and presumably not far from Whitehall, he *had* to have a headquarters but, other than hole-in-the-corner offices where we'd sometimes met, I'd never known the location of that headquarters. I didn't know whether he was married – I didn't know where the man lived ... I only knew that Jones was the man from whom I took orders and that, within limits, even *I* would be wise to obey those orders.

Which, as my cogitations grew slightly more involved, meant one very obvious thing. It meant that Sir Douglas Campbell was an industrialist with an uncommon amount of 'pull'.

They were thoughts – not particularly hairy thoughts – but they helped while away the time as I pushed south after the furniture van and Sir Douglas's favourite daughter.

We passed Sheffield on our right and Nottingham on our left; past Leicester then, at Junction 20, I followed the blip away from the motorway and east along the A247. We hit the A1 west of Peterborough then, for God's sake, we headed north again. It was bloody stupid. We were going *nowhere*.

I rang Jones to put him in the picture.

'You're sure about the van?'

'I'm sure about the van,' I growled.

'If the girl's in there ...'

'I don't have X-ray eyes, Jones. *Thompson's* in there. After that, it's educated guesswork.'

156

'Okay, if the girl *isn't* in there they'll lead you to her.'

'Jones,' I complained, 'they're zig-zagging around like a dog lost in a forest.'

'Fine. Zig-zag after them.'

'And if they're driving in shifts?'

'They can't go on for ever.'

'*I* can't go on for ever.'

He sneered, 'You're going soft in your old age,' and rang off.

That was the sort of boss he was. He kept you awake by making damn sure you hadn't time to sleep ... you were far too busy thinking up names for him!

Sunday, October 29th

2.30 a.m.

We were somewhere in the wilds of Lincolnshire. Somewhere south of Lincoln, somewhere east of Newark. Beyond that, I wouldn't have committed myself. The last road marking I'd seen was the B1202, and that had been some few miles back. I doubted that we were still on classified roads.

The blip was still on the screen and the van was still somewhere ahead. I'd found an all-night filling station not long since and I'd held the nozzle of the pump in the Merc's tank until the petrol had stopped on the automatic cut-out. I had the juice to follow them all night, if necessary, but it wasn't a prospect that had me warbling with delight. What is more, Lincolnshire is a notoriously billiard-table county and, a couple of times, I'd glimpsed the sweep of headlights ahead of me and, because they *might* have been the van's lights, I'd had to pull in and give the quarry a lengthening lead.

Ahead of me and in the cone of the Merc's beams it was as deserted as Outer Mongolia. Hedges, fields and the occasional solitary tree ... that, if you didn't count Thompson, who suddenly appeared, waving me to an unscheduled stop.

There was some slight cross-talk in which Thompson bared his teeth a little but, eventually, we were both in the Merc, racing after a blip on the screen which was rapidly reaching the outer limits of its range.

Thompson was in no mood for quiet conversation, and I was busy taking corners in pursuit of an unseen furniture van.

Then, having stared at the lifeless landscape which seems to stretch for ever in all directions, he spoke from his heart.

'Outer-bloody-Mongolia,' he muttered.

'Lincolnshire,' I corrected him, then added, 'But the same thought crossed *my* mind.'

2.45 a.m.

It ended. Not with a whimper, not with a bang, but with a call to the Merc's phone.

'Get back.' Jones's voice seemed to have a layer of permafrost.

'What?' I steered one-handed and scowled disbelief through the windscreen.

'It's all over.'

'What the hell!'

'The ransom's been paid. The girl's back with her father.'

'How the bloody hell can she be ...'

'*Get back!*' It was the first time I'd heard Jones shout

158

and the volume almost cracked an eardrum. Then, in a quieter tone, 'Rogate-on-Sands. Lyle's in this thing. It's where Thompson lives . . .'

'Thompson's here, with me,' I interrupted.

'That follows.' There was a hard grimness in the tone.

'Tomorrow.' I braked the Merc to the side of the road. 'Late, tomorrow afternoon. We'll find somewhere to spend the rest of the night.'

'Lyle's office, tomorrow afternoon at three. Be there, and bring Thompson along.'

THIRD
STAGE

Monday, October 30th

3.15 p.m.

The divisional headquarters at Rogate-on-Sands was a functional building, not yet ten years old. Almost by definition this meant it was neither outstanding nor ugly. Merely odd and out of place. The orange-coloured bricks with their quarter-of-an-inch-thick pointing showed evidence of architectural expertise far removed from that of the planners who had dreamed up the surrounding streets of solid, Victorian houses. The picture windows flooded the interior with light but, from outside, they looked flimsy alongside the heavy lintels of their neighbours. The all-glass swing-doors were clean and polished, but contrasted strangely with the solid oak of most other doors in the vicinity. The DHQ building had the only flat roof in sight.

It was a two-storey building, and Detective Chief Inspector Lyle's office was on the first floor; a large enough office for normal, everyday CID administrative work – indeed, some thought it too large – but today, and at this time, it seemed over-crowded.

Lyle had claimed his normal chair behind his desk. Other chairs had been brought into the office to accommodate the rest. Dilton-Emmet, Jones and Thompson were there. So was Gilliant. So was Liz Thompson. The stranger who completed the company was a well-built, well-dressed man whose lips seemed permanently on the point of moving into a mild, long-suffering smile. He had been introduced as 'from the Foreign Office' . . . but no more than that.

163

Gilliant was talking. He talked in a quiet, controlled drawl and, periodically, he glanced at the selection of the day's newspapers on the desk. The kidnapping and the recovery of Campbell's daughter claimed part of every front page.

'It is,' said Gilliant, 'the by now sorry story of kidnap-and-ransom insurance.' He seemed to be addressing his words directly at Harry and Liz Thompson. 'The business is booming. It has been for years.'

The two Thompsons looked slightly mystified.

'Kidnap-and-ransom insurance policies,' explained Gilliant. 'Since – to our certain knowledge, well over ten years ago – Lloyds have underwritten policies taken out by people – families – with a high risk factor of kidnap and ransom. They have always approved of firms like Control Risks Limited.'

'I'm sorry . . .' Thompson shook his head. 'I don't quite see . . .'

'More than a hundred policies in this country alone,' interrupted Gilliant. 'Almost five hundred throughout the world. Kidnap insurance. There's quite a scramble for clients, these days.'

'Is it *legal*?' Liz Thompson's eyes were wide as she asked the question.

'Legal,' sighed Gilliant, 'but not approved of. Get a man like Campbell. He takes out insurance against kidnap. It's a thing he *doesn't* want the police to know. His kid – his daughter – gets kidnapped. The terrorists – in this case, those trying for power in Shamoa . . .'

'Where the hell is Shamoa?' This time, Thompson dived in with the question. His puzzlement was tinged with a growing anger. 'What the blazes has . . .'

'Shamoa,' smiled the FO man, 'is one of the lesser African states, at present in some slight turmoil. The SIA have a . . .'

'The SIA?'

'The Shamoan Independence Army. Part military, part political. They . . .'

'They kidnapped Mary Campbell,' interposed Gilliant. 'They don't want the dam built. They also want money with which to finance some sort of revolution. That was the ransom. The cancellation of the dam project, plus a cool million. Campbell's paid the price.'

'Jesus wept!'

There was a silence before Dilton-Emmet spoke. The rumble of his words carried both disgust and some sympathy for both Thompson and his ex-wife.

He said, 'We've been played for suckers, old son. The old conjuring trick. As much movement as possible with the right hand, while the left hand quietly does all the clever stuff. Whichever outfit organised the pay-off also created a cover-up diversion to make sure *we* were racing up the wrong alley.'

'Not Control Risks,' murmured Gilliant. 'Sir Robert Mark wouldn't be part of a pantomime like this.'

'*Sir Robert Mark?*'

'A non-executive director,' smiled the FO man. 'It's *not* illegal.'

'And,' repeated Gilliant, 'we're quite sure Control Risks was *not* involved.'

'I – I still don't see who, or what . . .'

'Let *me* try.' Lyle leaned forward slightly and spoke directly to Harry and Liz Thompson. 'The Republic of Shamoa. A flea-bitten nation living on the poverty line – one of a hundred such states around the so-called Third World – and the president is a man called Hakim Al-Mokanna. A man who . . .'

'An absolute bastard,' grunted Dilton-Emmet.

'A man,' continued Lyle, patiently, 'who holds power by the skin of his teeth. His opponents are the SIA – the Shamoan Independence Army – and they just *might* overthrow Hakim Al-Mokanna if he makes a wrong move

. . . by which I mean an unpopular move.'

As Lyle paused, Thompson said, 'I'm damned if I see what all this has to do with . . .'

'Bear with me.' Lyle raised a hand a few inches from the desk top. He continued, 'Hakim – he likes to be called Hakim – Hakim has dreams of making his country prosperous, and one step towards national prosperity could come with the construction of a hydro-electric dam. That's where Sir Douglas Campbell and the Burns Civil Engineering Group – of which Sir Douglas is director general – comes in. *They* landed the contract for the building of the dam. Against stiff opposition, I might say.'

Again there was a pause but, by this time, Harry and Liz Thompson had been hooked by the intricacies of the tale and sat silent and waiting.

Lyle went on, 'The SIA *don't* want the dam. They argue that it will impoverish an already poor region of their nation. They also see the completion of the dam as a tacit seal of approval of Hakim Al-Mokanna's authority. If the dam gets built he'll be in power for the rest of his life.'

'So they – they kidnapped Campbell's daughter?' Thompson ran his fingers through his hair as he asked the tentative question.

'Just that.' Gilliant took up the tale and nodded. 'Which, in turn, brought in whichever kidnap-and-ransom insurance outfit Campbell is using. It was, it seems, *their* idea to set up a decoy fake-kidnap operation. To keep everybody occupied elsewhere.' The quick grin was both rueful and sympathetic. 'And we've all been "taken", Mr Thompson. We swallowed the bait, and we now look rather foolish.'

'Of all the . . .'

'It *wasn't* illegal. Dodgy . . . yes. Quite outrageous . . . I quite agree. But not *illegal*.'

'And,' added Dilton-Emmet, 'you *were* paid a thousand smackers a day for being the clown-dog.'

5.00 p.m.

All four men agreed that Harry and Liz Thompson
had believed the story. And why not? An explanation
solemnly offered by two senior police officers, a Foreign Office official and a duo from the dark corridors
of power like Jones and Dilton-Emmet carried more
than enough weight to silence a cheap private eye and
his ex-wife.

'Not a mention of Bankhurste.' The FO man voiced
the one sneaking doubt he still had. 'He saw him – he
saw he'd been murdered – but he never even mentioned
it.'

'A murder,' offered Gilliant. 'The local police are
handling it. Mr Lyle and I obviously know all about it.
Why mention it?'

All except the FO man had a beaker of hot, sweet
tea. The FO man had chosen unsweetened and unmilked
instant coffee. Lyle and Gilliant were smoking cigarettes.
Dilton-Emmet was smoking a cheroot.

The FO man said, 'Whatever else, nothing "international".'

'Are your lords and masters worried?' Jones had been
strangely quiet while the Thompsons had been with
them. Now, when he spoke, his voice was as cold and
brittle as thin ice. It showed a depth of anger unusual
in such a man. He sneered, 'Have you travelled all this
way to drop anchors?'

'Not at all.' The FO man was quite unperturbed.

'Because, if you seriously think . . .'

'I don't want to know,' smiled the FO man. 'Merely
make sure it doesn't become "international".'

Jones closed his mouth. The impression was that the
lips clamped together with an almost audible snap.

There was a period of vague silence; tea and coffee
were sipped, cigarettes and a cheroot were smoked and,

while the FO man seemed quite at ease, the hint of a quiver at his nostrils and the slightly knotted muscles of his jaw-line were evidence of Jones's almost uncontrollable fury.

They sat at a table of the Wine Bibber and worked hard to come to terms with what had happened and what they'd heard.

'To be such a sucker!' muttered Thompson.

'And the others,' soothed Liz.

'Yeah. I know. This bastard Campbell . . . the bloody "pull" he must have.'

'Cool it, my pet.' She moved her hand and placed it over his on the top of the table.

From behind the bar counter Bull Adams watched and approved. He couldn't hear the conversation. Nevertheless, he decided that externals seemed to point to some sort of reconciliation. He grinned to himself, reached for a bottle behind the bar and poured two glasses of one of the best wines he kept in stock. He carried them to the table and placed one in front of Thompson and one in front of the ex-Mrs Thompson.

'On the house.' He smiled.

He left before they had time to thank him.

'What the hell?' Thompson stared at Adams's retreating back.

'He's a good friend.' Liz tasted the wine. 'That's something Jerry Bankhurste *wasn't*.'

'Jerry's dead,' grunted Thompson.

'You *think* he's dead.'

'Eh?'

'They've led you by the nose in so many things. That could be one more trick they've played.'

'Who? Who are "they"?'

'The men we've just left. Campbell. The insurance crowd. The Shamoan revolutionaries. Take your pick.

They've *all* been plucking your feathers, boy.'

'It would seem so.' Thompson sipped at the wine. 'Dammit . . . *anything!*'

'Anything at all,' she agreed, quietly. Then, 'Harry, my love, you need a keeper.'

Thompson scowled irritable embarrassment at the glass of wine.

'You are *not* a very good detective,' she said gently.

The scowl darkened.

'You're an even worse investigative journalist.'

'Look – for God's sake – I . . .'

'You're not a bad *newshound*,' insisted Liz, 'but you're not tough enough for the other thing. Not ruthless enough.' Then, with a touch of impatience in her tone, 'Good grief, man! That's meant as a *compliment.*'

'Yeah. I know.' The grin was both wry and bitter. 'I need a keeper. '

'You're a good man, Harry. A nice man.' Her fingers squeezed his hand gently. 'Like so many things. People don't know *how* good until it's too late.'

'Liz . . .' He swallowed, then muttered, 'Give it time, my love. Give it time, then maybe. At the moment – y'know – we have a very sweet arrangement. Let's leave it at that . . . for now.' He paused, lowered his chin onto his chest and, in a tiny voice, continued, 'I'm scared, Liz. That's the truth of it. I don't want to screw it up again. Not *again.* Just – y'know . . . give it time.'

'Till for ever,' she whispered.

He seemed to pull himself together, grinned, shrugged then said, 'Y'know who I *really* feel sorry for?'

She shook her head.

'The son – Alex – he seemed such a nice guy. I mean, even if he gets over the loss of memory bit, he'll carry that scar on his face for life.'

169

Tuesday, October 31st

12.30 a.m.

The four schemers – Jones, Dilton-Emmet, Gilliant and Lyle – still waited. The FO man had left.

'I'm sorry. I have a train to catch.'

'You have also a despatch rider to *miss*,' Dilton-Emmet had growled.

The FO man had broadened the knowing smile, which seemed part of his permanent expression, had not replied and had caught his train.

Later, the quartet had left the headquarters building for a quick meal at a nearby Indian restaurant. It had been a strange meal; a strangely silent meal and the silence had been one of suppressed fury coupled with the knowledge that they were all tacitly committed to a line of action which, if things went wrong, could, at the very least, land them in a criminal dock.

Gilliant had said, 'I only hope the Special Branch know their job.'

'They know how to search.' Jones's comeback had been immediate and impatient. 'They'll have a warrant. They'll tear the place to kindling wood, if necessary.'

That had been more than four hours ago, and now they were awaiting the arrival of the despatch rider. The search had been a success. That much they already knew. How much of a success they were waiting to learn.

The office was thick with smoke. The ash-trays were nests of used matches and cigarette and cheroot ends. Beakers of scummed tea made the desk and the top of a steel filing cabinet look untidy and uncared for.

Lyle put his hand to his mouth to kill a yawn, stretched his arms, then hoisted himself from his chair. He strolled to the window and stared, unseeing, at the street lighting.

170

'Too smooth,' he mused. 'We should have spotted it
... it was *far* too smooth.'

'You sensed it ... remember?' grunted Dilton-Emmet.

'I sensed *something*. I didn't know what.'

'Just because there isn't a complete cock-up,' snapped
Jones, irritably, 'that doesn't mean ...'

'There's always *something* of a cock-up.'

'Speak for yourself, Chief Inspector.'

'Speak for all of us,' drawled Gilliant, soothingly.
'All except Bankhurste. He was wise. That's why they're
burying him.'

'At a guess,' observed Lyle, 'with Bankhurste dead, and
when the news of a Special Branch search of his home
leaks out, there'll be a few sweaty palms in high places.'
He tilted his head and looked down to the street, then
continued, 'The waiting time is over, gentlemen. The
despatch rider is just pulling into the forecourt.'

Sunday, November 5th

10.30 a.m.

The grey-suited official led Gilliant and Lyle along
the heavily carpeted corridor, towards Campbell's private
office. The corridor had no windows, but concealed lighting made it like day and illuminated the series of framed
examples of modern art which cancelled the severity of
the walls.

The official tapped on the panel before opening the
door and standing aside in order to allow the two officers
to enter. As the door closed Sir Douglas Campbell rose
from a chair behind the desk and motioned towards the

171

two similar chairs which had been strategically placed, facing him across the desk.

It was some desk! In surface area it was only slightly less than a table-tennis table. Glass-topped, with a gilt surround. It seemed almost a criminal waste of space upon which to house a telephone, an intercom speaker, a giant ash-tray and a massive, leather-bound blotter. A picture window took up most of the wall behind Campbell's chair and through it Lyle could see the Telecom Tower in the near-distance. No sound of London's traffic found its way into *this* office.

It was, indeed, some desk . . . and *some* office!

As Lyle was later to remark, 'The Hitler thing. Something of a short-arse out to impress – out to demonstrate his power and, at the same time, intimidate – by the size of his desk and the yards of carpet you needed to cross before you come to within speaking distance.'

But that was later. On this Bonfire Day morning Campbell sensed he had met his match. That, to these solemn-faced officers, neither bare boards nor best Axminster was going to make much difference.

The two officers sat down, and only then did Campbell resume his seat. He stared, first at Gilliant then at Lyle, then he touched the inch-thick file which sat, closed, on the desk blotter.

'This,' he said. 'I take it you think it's true?'

'We *know* it's true,' said Gilliant, calmly.

'You have more faith in this muck-raker, Bankhurste, than I have.'

'All you have there,' explained Gilliant, 'are photo-copies of the originals. And not *all* the originals, by a long chalk. We've also made our own enquiries. Checked and double-checked. Taken statements. All in all, obtained more than enough firm confirmation. What you've read there is true, all right. We can take that as a starting point.'

'I see.' Campbell leaned back in his chair.

'A few questions, then,' continued Gilliant.

'If you know all the answers, why ask the questions?'

'If,' said Lyle, quietly, '*you* think we don't know the answers, why are *you* here?'

'Do I need my solicitor?' asked Campbell.

'No.' Gilliant shook his head.

'Would you tell me, if I did?'

'Of course. We daren't risk *not* telling you.'

'Good.' Campbell allowed a tight smile to move across his lips. 'At least we're agreed on one thing. You're not questioning some grubby little sneak-thief.'

'There is,' drawled Gilliant, 'nothing grubby about anybody who works from an office like this.'

'But . . . still a thief?' Campbell matched tone for tone.

'Thieving?' said Gilliant, thoughtfully. 'A difficult activity to define. You waste your life . . . have you stolen your own life? It's yours. *Can* you steal it? Not in law, of course. But, morally, does that make you a thief? A particularly stupid thief? Because of you, somebody else's life has been wasted. Does *that* make you a thief? A thief of time, perhaps? Some other person's time?'

'That's very deep.' Campbell's tone carried a hint of contempt. 'Very erudite. Does it *mean* anything?'

'Somebody else's honesty.' Gilliant continued as if Campbell hadn't spoken. 'Somebody else's honour. A theft . . . surely? A particularly disgusting form of thieving. The theft of a nation's honour. Of its right to freedom.'

'Based on this?' Campbell glanced at the file in front of him. 'Based on the crap that Bankhurste digs up?'

'*Dug* up,' corrected Gilliant. 'Past tense. He's no longer with us.'

'I've heard.'

'You *know*.'

Campbell wouldn't be drawn.

'Let's talk about kidnapping,' suggested Gilliant.

Campbell shrugged.

'Specifically, let's talk about *non*-kidnapping. About a neat little idea meant to waste a lot of valuable time and point a lot of noses in the wrong direction.'

'Valuable time?' mocked Campbell. 'Let us also not forget that *I* paid out good money. Quite a lot of good money.'

It was a technique as old as policing. It was time-wasting guyed up as sly and careful interrogation. Gilliant and Lyle were experts at the game and, when Gilliant ran out of subject-matter, Lyle would take over. Between them, and with their combined skills, they could keep Campbell anchored all day.

There was no time difference between the United Kingdom and Shamoa. The watches of Jones and Dilton-Emmet showed the same o'clock as the watches of Gilliant and Lyle.

The two pairs had little else in common.

Sweat patches stained the shirts, down the spine and under the armpits of Jones and the bearded giant as they moved as quickly as possible between the clap-board and corrugated-iron dwellings of the poorer quarter. An open drain ran down the middle of the unmade road and sent the smell of its filth up to attract thousands of flies. Occasionally scavenger birds lifted themselves awkwardly off some unidentifiable and half-eaten offal as they approached. Pot-bellied kids, frightened-eyed women and sullen-faced men noted their passing from the darkness of sack-curtained doorways or from narrow side-turnings.

It was oven-hot and stinking. The big man yanked an already damp bandana from the hip pocket of his shorts and mopped his face and beard.

'Al-Mokanna's "Brave New World",' he growled, disgustedly.

'I've known worse places.'

174

'Of course. Me, too . . . but not many and not much.'

A few minutes later a voice called softly from one of the narrow side-streets.

'Jones, sir.'

The skinny, bare-footed, teenage youth was dressed in a torn shirt and khaki shorts. The wide grin showed perfect teeth as he motioned Jones and Dilton-Emmet to follow him into the web of alleys and cul-de-sacs.

11.00 a.m.

Campbell was talking. He was bragging a little, but that didn't matter. Like a dripping tap filling a bowl, he was filling time with words.

'. . . despite the name. I'm no part of the Clan Campbell, nor want to be. Some few years back one of the academic types dug around. I didn't ask him. He offered to do the job and I let him get on with it. The wrong side of the blanket . . . that's how far he got. Some stupid little crofter's daughter. An unmarried tart who called her bastard "Danny Campbell", for no better reason than it had to have some sort of name.

'That's how we started. Since then, we've kept the name. We've married Englishwomen, we've married colleens, we've married Jewesses. *Everything!* But always a male heir to carry the name into the next generation. And always businessmen. Always *good* businessmen.'

'Quite a dynasty,' murmured Lyle.

'Don't mock, Chief Inspector.' Campbell's eyes narrowed. 'Don't take the piss out of success. Let me tell you something. A few things. Blind Jack Metcalf of Knaresborough. Telford. McAdam. Brindley. Even Brunel. The canals, the bridges, the railways. It was all pick-and-shovel work in those days. All *man*-power. Raw *muscle*-power. The egg-heads gawp at the Pyramids

175

and wonder how in hell *they* were built. They're blind to what's on their own doorstep. A hundred miles of tunnels driven through hillside and mountains. A thousand miles of canals, complete with locks. The bridges, the viaducts, the railway cuttings. Christ Almighty! *We* did that ... much of it. We provided the men, we provided the tools – what little tools they had – we organised the labour.

'That's what *my* family organised, Chief Inspector Lyle. Without lorries, without any of the modern paraphernalia. Sledge-hammers and crowbars ... that's all. Without what *we* did there wouldn't have *been* an Industrial Revolution ...'

Dilton-Emmet removed the sacking, then the oiled silk, from the Savage. It was a .303 Model 99 lever-action repeating carbine. It was in mint condition. A Carl Zeiss 'Jena' telescopic sight had been carefully added.

'Almost a museum piece,' observed the big man.

'Jones, sir.' The rag-wrapped man who spoke looked suddenly worried. It was there in the lowered brows above the veined eyes. His near-black features were far too lined to allow a mere frown to crumple them further. He said, 'Jones, sir, it is a good gun. It is new. A man could not wish for a better gun.'

'It's a good gun,' soothed Jones.

Dilton-Emmet worked the lever action of the carbine, then held the gun up to squint through the telescopic sight.

'A good gun,' he agreed, at last. Then, 'How far to the balcony? Do we know?'

'Sir, two hundred and fourteen paces.' The youth who had guided them to the room answered. 'I have paced it. Three times I have paced it. Two hundred and fourteen paces.'

The big man grunted his satisfaction then, still holding the Savage, stepped up onto the makeshift firing step, tested the steadiness of the sandbags stacked into an elbow rest, then peered through the irregular, six-inch hole which had been punched through the wall of the shack.

'Trick shooting,' he observed drily.

'Sir.' The youth grinned his usual accompaniment to a remark and held out his open hand. 'I have made them very special bullets. Jones, sir, explained.'

The four rounds of British Army issue .303 ammunition had been cleaned, polished then doctored. The noses had been filed flat, then a tiny cross had been scored into the flattened surfaces.

'Sir, they are – what you say? – bang-bang.'

'Dum-dum.' Dilton-Emmet took the rounds and eyed them. He glanced at Jones, and grunted, 'Not *too* tricky, after all.'

'Anywhere above the crotch,' said Jones calmly. 'They'll have to hose his innards off the balcony floor.'

11.30 a.m.

' . . . and my grandfather founded the organisation I now run. My father expanded it and I, in turn, have turned it into a close-knit group of companies with a regular annual turnover of something well in excess of two billion pounds. Alex will take over from me, when I retire.'

'You also have a daughter.' Lyle made the gentle observation while, at the same time, seeming to concentrate his attention upon the distant Telecom Tower beyond the window.

'Mary? Yes, of course. She's . . .'

'She wasn't kidnapped.'

'You people!' Campbell's lips curled slightly. 'A mild, but necessary, ploy. A comparatively harmless wild goose chase. And what happens? Your ego is such that you . . .'

'No, forgive me, Sir Douglas.' Lyle's interruption was deceptively polite. With equal politeness, he continued, 'I'm not talking about those few days when Mr Thompson was led by the nose to all four points of the compass. I'm talking about your daughter, Mary. Your *real* daughter. She was *not* kidnapped. She has *never* been kidnapped.'

'Chief Inspector, I have a cool million reasons for calling you a liar.'

'Come, now.' Lyle foreshortened the focus of his eyes and stared Campbell in the face. 'We have a signed statement from your daughter. We have a signed statement from the school-friend she stayed with. We have statements from her other friends, who all view it as a great joke. We have . . .'

'We have *statements*,' cut in Gilliant. 'Enough statements *not* to waste our time trying to bluff. Bankhurste knew enough to draw the skeleton. We've merely fleshed it out.'

Campbell sat and waited.

'Well?' Gilliant dropped the one-word question into the silence.

'Am I being charged?' Cambell's question was hard, but soft-spoken. 'Am I to *be* charged?'

'Not today. Not by us.'

Lyle added, 'The DPP, perhaps . . . if he can find something to fit a very unusual situation.'

'He'll find something,' muttered Campbell bitterly.

'It's not impossible.'

'Bankhurste is not our problem,' explained Gilliant, teasingly.

'Bankhurste?' The eyes glittered with sudden suspicion.

'Whoever shot him.'

'Has he *been* shot?'

'Oh, yes. Murdered.'

'I wouldn't know. I steer clear of the tabloids.'

Gilliant chuckled, quietly. It was a soft noise, but filled

178

with meaning. It called Campbell a liar without the need for words.

'We are,' said Lyle, 'here purely in the interest of personal curiosity. We're police officers. We like tidy answers, no matter how complicated the questions.' He moved one shoulder in the hint of a resigned shrug. 'If we've been made to look a little foolish, so be it . . . it won't be the first time. But there has to be a reason. With a man like you, there has to be a *good* reason. A reason why the newspapers – including the tabloids – carried a story about the kidnapping of your daughter, when she hadn't *been* kidnapped. A reason for an involved – not to say expensive – game of follow-my-leader in which dust was very successfully thrown into the eyes of fools and wise men alike. A reason. . . for *everything*.'

'We'd like to know,' added Gilliant. 'I'm sure Jones, too, would like to know.'

'Jones, sir.' The old man with the wrinkled face hesitated. Then he asked the question. 'Jones, sir, why *you*?'

Jones smiled pretended puzzlement.

'Why *you*, sir?' insisted the old man. 'We, too, have men who can shoot rifles. Good men. Good marksmen. Some have lived with a rifle by their side since they were boys. Why *you*, Jones, sir?'

'Are they laughed at?' asked Jones, quietly. 'Are they made to look foolish? These men with rifles . . . are they made to look like stupid women?'

'Oh no, Jones, sir.' The old man shook his head with great solemnity. 'To make them look foolish would be very dangerous.'

'I, too, am such a man.' Jones glanced to where the boy was standing on the firing step, keeping watch. He said, 'The soldiers? Have they arrived?'

'The vehicles with the ordinary soldiers are arriving, Jones, sir. The special soldiers who parade in front of

179

the palace are not yet there. The parade ground is empty.'

'They will come, Jones, sir,' the old man assured him. 'Al-Mokanna prides himself upon being a ruler not unlike your own monarch. His special troops – his bodyguard – must be seen. Their discipline must be apparent. This first Sunday in each month he must make his demonstration. His vanity demands these things, Jones, sir.'

'Vanity.' Jones nodded, slowly. 'I, too, am vain.'

'Peter?' Campbell smiled. It was a sly, self-satisfied smile. He said, 'Peter Jones? The great trickster? One of those shadowy Establishment figures everybody is a little frightened of. I know Peter Jones, Chief Constable. I know him rather well.'

'Really?' Gilliant made believe mild interest.

'As much as any man,' claimed Campbell. 'I've dined with him. Played bridge with him. He's a cunning player. A cunning conversationalist.' The smile grew until it became a gentle laugh. 'Part of this whole business was to make Peter Jones look a little foolish. To demonstrate his shortcomings. To prove that even *he* can be out-smarted.'

'All this expense.' Gilliant put on a look of surprise. 'All this back-door horse-trading – your son, your daughter, God only knows who else . . . just to put one over on Jones?'

'Good God, no!' And now Campbell was serious. Very serious and very intent. He leaned forward slightly. 'The dam, Gilliant. The Shamoan dam. The firm needs that dam. It needs that dam even more than Al-Mokanna needs it.'

'Economically?' suggested Lyle, softly.

'What other reason is there?' Campbell's mood had changed. The hint of a glare made his eyes gleam. 'This

180

is a jungle, Chief Inspector. No second prizes. You either win or you lose. And we can't afford to lose. We *need* that blasted dam.'

'Otherwise you . . . "lose"?'

'Otherwise, we lose,' said Campbell flatly.

'Everything?' pressed Lyle.

'In effect.'

Lyle pursed his lips, then murmured, 'You must have some very inefficient financial advisers, Sir Douglas.'

'What?'

'Every egg in the same basket. That's not very wise.'

'What the hell do *you* know about business?'

'Not a lot,' admitted Lyle.

'In that case . . .' Campbell closed his mouth then, in a calmer tone, continued, 'It's the game, Lyle. It makes roulette look like buying apples. That's what it's all *about*. The calculated risk. The carefully worked out gamble.'

'Not the careful way?' teased Lyle. 'Not the "Lever" way? The "EMI" way?'

'Chicken-hearted conglomerates,' sneered Campbell.

'Go for broke, every time?'

'That's *my* way. It's always been *my* way.'

In a voice as soft as a kitten's paw, Gilliant murmured, 'Ergo – a million-quid nest egg makes for personal stability . . . am I right?'

11.45 a.m.

Dilton-Emmet had replaced the boy on the firing step. He watched the activities around the presidential palace while, at the same time, listening to the talk within the room.

Jones said, 'The Shamoan Independence people. They're in position?'

'Jones, sir.' The old man sounded almost hurt at having to answer the question. 'The barracks. They have already taken over the barracks. Quietly. Without fuss. Much of the army – many of the commanders – are on our side. Units known to favour Al-Mokanna are away on manoeuvres. Patrol duty. Anything. They will be able to do nothing until it is too late.'

The boy added, 'We here are safe, Jones, sir. All within a hundred yards of here are SIA sympathisers.'

'It won't be bloodless,' warned Jones. 'It's a finely balanced thing.'

'A monster without a head?' The old man's creaky chuckle held confidence. 'As useless as a hooded hawk, Jones, sir.'

'It may not be able to see,' growled Jones. 'But it still has beak and talons.'

The army units surrounding the palace and the parade square were in position. Armoured cars and lorries, and uniformed men standing, firm-footed in their heavy boots. Backs to the presidential headquarters and forming a first line of defence against any spontaneous uprising. SMGs slung from their shoulders and at the ready.

Jones repeated, 'It won't be bloodless, old man. Come noon, there'll be bullets galore flying.'

Campbell was sweating. Not droplets, not even pinheads, but enough to bring the hint of a sheen to his upper lip. Which meant Campbell was worried – maybe even scared – and both Gilliant and Lyle were professionals enough to read the signs.

'It's your money,' said Gilliant, off-handedly. 'It's *your* million.'

Campbell nodded.

'Some Accounting Section,' observed Lyle.

Campbell looked a pretend question.

'A million coming in,' explained Lyle. 'By the time

they've fixed the books it reads like a million going out.'

'Slip a few zeroes in the wrong column, Chief Inspector.' Gilliant made it sound as if he knew every angle known to man. 'A plus sign here to read like a minus sign there. It's done all the time . . . right, Campbell?'

'Perhaps I do need my solicitor,' said Campbell in a slightly hoarse tone.

'Not unless you've done something *dishonest*,' said Gilliant.

'Nothing dishonest.' Campbell cleared his throat. 'I assure you, gentlemen. Nothing *dishonest* . . . as *you* understand that word.'

'Has it more than one meaning ?' asked Lyle, innocently.

'Business acumen.'

'Ah!' Lyle nodded understanding. '*Business* acumen.'

'Meaning,' said Gilliant, 'the ancient and honourable ploy of you-scratch-my-back-I'll-scratch-yours.'

'It's done all the time,' breathed Campbell. 'Every big international contract that was ever negotiated. The wheels have to be oiled. The men at the heart of the negotiations are always . . .'

'*In the other direction* . . . surely?' interrupted Gilliant.

'What?' Campbell looked genuinely puzzled.

Gilliant said, 'A large organisation – an organisation similar to your own – goes into competition for a major contract. Let's say a dam, let's say a bridge, let's say *anything*. Those offering the contract, especially if they're Middle East types, have their own code of conduct. Greasing palms – it's not called that, but that's what it boils down to – is accepted "business acumen" as you care to call it. It happens . . . always. Those offering the contract *expect* a back-hander. It's an accepted under-the-counter part of the deal. Very often the contract is, in effect, *bought*.'

Campbell moved his head in a tiny nod.

'But not *this* time.' Gilliant's eyes held those of Campbell in a steady, not-to-be-denied gaze. 'This time, the kick-back comes in the *opposite* direction. From the contractor to the firm picking up the contract. From the country putting out the contract to the firm picking up the contract. It's like water running uphill. It doesn't make sense. That's why we're here, Campbell. To find out *why* it makes sense.'

'The plus signs and the minus signs,' added Lyle, gently. 'They're in the wrong place. *Why?*'

Campbell moistened his lips. The sheen on his upper lip was more obvious. It was augmented by tiny points of sweat on his forehead.

'Do you object to me smoking?' he croaked.

Gilliant said, 'It's your office.'

Campbell slipped a cigar case from his inside pocket. He snipped the end of the cigar with a gold-plated contraption. He flicked a lighter into flame and rolled the end of the cigar in the flame, then returned the lighter to his pocket. He enjoyed a lungful of expensive tobacco smoke and when he began his explanation he had recovered his composure. He was, once more, the high-flying industrialist. The man at the helm of a massive civil engineering concern. This time, there was no hesitation. No hint of apology. Only a man of power explaining the manner in which that power was manipulated.

'It is, you see,' he began, 'rather simple. Not too involved at all, when the facts are known and understood . . .'

The Palace Guard – the élite of the soldiery, Al-Mokanna's carefully chosen personal bodyguard – were marching into view on the parade square. They were smart and they moved well. They were paid to obey orders, without question. They were paid to form a human wall between Al-Mokanna and anybody wishing to do him harm. They were paid to die rather than allow anything to happen to their master.

They were paid well and, because of what they were, the laws of Shamoa could never reach them.

Dilton-Emmet reached an arm out and, without taking his eyes from the parade square, closed his fingers around the Savage carbine. The young boy had already fed cartridges into the magazine and a single movement of the lever slammed a round into the breech.

'. . . Al-Mokanna and I want the same thing. The dam. With the dam he will be safe in office. The Western world will see Shamoa as a nation eager to shake off the trappings of tribal primitiveness. The various financial institutions will feel more able to invest in the country. It is a perpetuating situation, gentlemen. These things always are. The trigger is the dam . . .'

Dilton-Emmet poked the snout of the Savage out through the aperture in the wall, nestled his cheek against the stock and squinted through the telescopic sight.

He was an old hand at the game. He knew his body needed as much oxygen as possible for a rock-steady shot, therefore he began to take deep and rhythmic breaths. Extra rounds were in the magazine, but he was professional enough to want to perform a clean, single-shot execution.

'. . . The fly in the ointment, of course, is the so-called Shamoan Independence Army. The SIA. As far as Al-Mokanna is concerned, the SIA have *always* been the fly in the ointment.

'African politics – I don't have to tell you about African politics – but in Shamoa it just about drives any reasonable person crazy. "The Opposition" means the guy who's going to bury you, given half a chance, therefore you bury *him* first . . . if *you* get half a chance. And the SIA have a rather efficient propaganda set-up. Good enough to make HM Government tend to side with *them*. Not openly, of course – the Whitehall crowd always genuflect towards the man whose head is stamped on the coinage – but in a thousand and one little behind-the-back ways. That's why the pressure was on me not to put in a bid for the dam project. The present Shamoan government – meaning Al-Mokanna – wanted it. The SIA *didn't* want it, and Whitehall leaned towards the anti-Al-Mokanna faction.

'It became necessary to discredit the SIA . . .'

'The radio station?' Jones's question was low-pitched.

'Jones, sir!' The old man's tone carried gentle resentment. He continued, 'The radio station, the telephone exchange, the government offices. They are *ours*, Jones, sir. All key installations are there for the taking. Our men are *there*, waiting for noon.'

'They won't have long to wait,' grunted Jones.

Noon

Al-Mokanna was wearing a tailored battle-dress. It looked very smart and the double-row of ribbons on the left breast contrasted with the jungle-green and brown of the camouflage pattern. The wine-coloured beret sported a flying-eagle badge which, at a distance, might have been mistaken for a British paratrooper's badge. Perhaps it was meant to be so mistaken.

As he stepped through the french windows and onto the balcony the band, immediately below, struck up the Shamoan national anthem and the officer in charge of

186

the bodyguard brought the troops to a moderately smart attention.

Dilton-Emmet viewed the Shamoan leader through the magnification of the telescopic sight and noted certain faults in the cut of the battledress blouse.

He muttered, 'Damn the man. He's wearing a flak-vest.'

Jones and the two Shamoan nationals watched the big man, but remained silent.

Dilton-Emmet tilted the snout of the carbine until the sight's cross-wires were lined upon Al-Mokanna's mouth. It was a more difficult shot, but the stock of the weapon was smooth against his cheek and firm against his shoulder muscle. Because it was a tricky shot there was no time for hesitation. The target was motionless and would remain so until the end of the national anthem.

He squeezed the trigger with a slow but firm pressure.

The explosion seemed to coincide with the sudden bursting of Al-Mokanna's head. The two men who flanked, and were slightly behind, were literally sprayed with blood, brain-tissue and shattered bone.

Quite calmly, Dilton-Emmet stepped down from the shooting position and handed the carbine to the boy.

He said, 'Messy . . . but very certain.'

From outside the room the noise of rising mob panic gave an indication of what was happening. Already the stutter of SMGs punctuated the shouting.

'Come, Jones, sir.' The old man beckoned with some degree of urgency. 'We have transport ready. The air-strip will be in our hands when we arrive.'

'. . . it became necessary to paint the SIA as terrorists.'

'Hence the kidnapping?' murmured Gilliant.

'Hence the *fake* kidnapping,' corrected Campbell. 'A young, out-of-work actress, a handful of Al-Mokanna's own men.'

'To say nothing of a handful of suckers.'

187

'Including senior police officers and government officials,' added Lyle, coldly.

'I took legal advice.' Campbell drew on the cigar. 'I'm told I did nothing illegal.'

'Murder?' Gilliant raised a questioning eyebrow.

'Sad about Bankhurste,' smiled Campbell.

'We think he was getting close,' said Gilliant, coldly.

'Close?'

'Close to what you were up to. Close to the involved game of puss-in-the-corner you and Al-Mokanna were playing. Close enough to require his removal.'

'I didn't kill him, Chief Constable.'

'Of course not. Capone wasn't one of the gunners at the St Valentine's Day Massacre.'

'I'm not a gangster, Gilliant.'

'No?' This time Lyle asked the question which called Campbell a liar. 'There's a million quid. One cool million . . . and it's disappeared. One million in ransom money . . . but there's been no kidnapping. In a Swiss bank somewhere? In a numbered account?'

'Chief Inspector, you've been reading too many crime novels.'

'Without that dam project,' continued Lyle, 'you – this organisation you head – goes down the john.' Then, as Campbell made to speak, 'Don't waste time on denials. That's the one fact Bankhurste could prove up to the hilt. The one thing *we* can prove up to the hilt.'

'Risks are necessary,' sighed Campbell. 'In business – in this wicked world – with German, American and Japanese firms all jostling to get the big contracts. It's dog eats dog, Lyle. The risk has to be taken.'

'With a nice, million-quid safety net to ensure your own personal survival.'

Campbell smiled.

'In a nutshell,' drawled Gilliant. 'That dam project is a life or death gamble for the Burns Civil Engineering

Group. The Al-Mokanna faction favour the dam project, but the SIA faction would cancel the project.'

'And of course,' said Campbell, 'the British Government aren't wildly enthusiastic about *anybody*, but of two unknown evils favour the SIA if only because they have had a certain amount of experience with the Al-Mokanna regime.'

Lyle said, 'They could be mistaken ... the UK Government, I mean.'

'I deal in civil engineering, Lyle. Politics don't interest me.'

'In other words, you don't care?' said Gilliant.

'Right.' Campbell nodded.

'Which,' added Gilliant, flatly, 'is as good a reason as any for faking a kidnapping, plastering some of the less reputable news-rags with headlines accusing the SIA of terrorist tactics ... and, as a by-product, pocketing a nice little tax-free nest egg in case things come unstuck.'

'I faked a kidnapping,' said Campbell carefully. 'Beyond that ... you're guessing, Gilliant.' He seemed to ponder for a moment while he drew on the cigar, then he said, 'What would *really* make the SIA a terrorist outfit would be the assassination of Al-Mokanna ... there, of course, being a Number Two ready and eager to step into his shoes.'

main

C.1

M